Blackstone County

Mission One

E. B. Payne

ISBN: 9780692052426

Physical Area of Story

Blackstone County, North Carolina

Stonehope – Town in Blackstone County

Blackstone – A Huge, Ancient Granite Boulder

Webbs Mill – Blackstone Grist Mill

Main Characters

Dale Weaver – Federation of Planets Cadet

E. H. Denton – Patriarch of Denton Family

Stanley Hall – Paramedic and Secret Agent

Vernon Maddox – Sheriff of Blackstone County

Other Characters

Agnes Maddox – Sister of Vernon Maddox

Brutus – Name of Drug Kingpin

Cooksey – Cook at Edwards Diner

Cotton – Worker at Stonehouse Farm

Detective Cain – Blackstone Sheriff's Office

Detective Perez – Blackstone Sheriff's Office

Dorothy Webb – Sister of E. H. Denton

Dwight Gacy – Paramedic

E. H. Denton – Owner of Denton Farm

Inrun52 (Miss Tetterton) – Secret Agent

Johnny Edwards – Owner of Edwards Diner

Jordon Denton – Grandson of E. H. Denton

Other Characters Continued

Junior Maddox – Son of Vernon Maddox

Katherine Denton – Daughter-in-law of E. H. Denton

Larry Denton – Son of E. H. Denton

Mad Dog – Works for Junior Maddox

Martin Webb – Brother-in-law of E. H. Denton

Miss Tetterton (Inrun52) – Stanley Hall's Handler

Mozart – Dale Weaver's Dog

Ms. Marshall – Receptionist at Community College

Officer Jackson – Deputy Blackstone Sheriff's Department

Pam Mann – Waitress at Edwards Diner

Pearl James – Housekeeper

Ratchet – E. H. Denton's Dog

Rex Moore – Cadet of Federation of Planets

Rodney Medlin – Owner of Medlin's Garage

Rooster – Church Function Cook

Sarah Denton – Wife of E. H. Denton

Skylar Denton – Granddaughter of E. H. Denton

Stephen Denton – Nephew of E. H. Denton

Sunny Tupelo – Hometown Girl and Actress

Teddy Mann – Son of Pam Mann

The-Man – Stonehouse Farm Manager

Vernel Maddox – Pearl James' Daughtry

EPISODE 1

Dale sat in the Sonoran Desert cross-legged amidst the organ pipe cacti which loomed above him. He looked upward at the Arizona afternoon sky as he scanned for any signs of his transport.

The last five years had been as Dale's orders. He had successfully followed the drug trail to North Carolina, and he had the scars to prove it, physically and mentally.

His mission had taken him and his partner, Rex Moore, deep undercover in one of the most active drug cartels in the world. The Federation chose Dale and Rex because of their natural dark skin and their learned Hispanic language. It gave them an advantage after disembarking a few miles west of the Tohono O'odham Indian Reservation in a remote desert area of Arizona.

Dale and Rex had hiked the five miles from the disembark area to Ajo to find the La Siesta Motel and RV Resort. Dale carried an RV key, an Arizona driver's license, and his passport, and Rex held an electronic car key, an Arizona driver's license as well, and his passport.

Both passports revealed they had previously been in the United States, Mexico, Columbia, Canada, and several other South American countries, all untrue. It was their first Federation mission and their first arrival.

Dale was sitting on the same spot, the exact GPS coordinates as he had done five years ago. His hair was still bushy and his black beard out of control.

Only Rex was not there. At first, the two young men were flippant concerning the danger and seriousness of their assignment.

They were both twenty-three, muscle-bound, trained to fight and to survive almost any situation. Dale now could look back and see their greenhorn mistakes, the mistakes which cost Rex his life.

Dale was given the name Luis Angel Alveraz, and for Rex, the name Juan Vega Romero was given. Although they were not related to each other, they came into their assignment as cousins, and their features seemed to confirm they were family.

Not only had Dale and Rex trained together, but they had been together since they were born. They thought of each other as brothers.

Dale reminisced about how he and Rex trained to pilot go-fast boats and small cargo submarines. With a background meticulously built on the internet, they only had to wait to be contacted by a cartel lieutenant. They were to meet him in Belize at the Island Magic Beach Resort.

He and Rex had been at the resort a week and a half before being contacted. Although Dale had been approached earlier by a slim blond wearing a barely-there bikini, he sat alone. It was late in the afternoon, and as usual, Rex had taken a beautiful young girl to their room.

As Dale sat nursing a beer, he positioned himself so he could look towards the breaking waves. After about an hour, he saw him again. The dark-skinned man who stood over six feet tall walked towards Dale wearing a bathing suit and dark sunglasses.

Dale had noticed the man the first day they were there and every day since. He was always well dressed, but this was the first time he had seen him on the beach.

Dale watched as the toned man walked about three hundred yards past the sunbathers. Then, he turned and retraced his footsteps until he began walking towards the beach bar.

Dale kept his eyes on the stranger as he came closer. He walked up to Dale and said, "Senior Alveras, you have been watching me."

"Don't like surprises; been watching you every day."

"Yes, I am aware," said the stranger in a Columbian solid accent. "I see Senior Romero pleases himself with a woman again."

Dale looked into the dark eyes of his guest and then studied his beer as he said, "Si."

The tall man reached into his bathing suit pocket, pulled out an envelope, and handed it to Dale, saying, "Your instructions are here." He smiled, turned, and began making his way toward the main entrance of the resort.

In hindsight, Dale knew that day was the beginning of Rex's demise. As it had been since Rex died, Dale was thinking of all the ways he could have saved his brother.

As he was staring at a giant Organ Pipe cactus, he replayed the scenarios until he saw the glint of light reflect off of his transport. He was soon in the air and on his way to the next position. Only this time, he was alone.

The flight did not take him to his next mission area right away but to the Yucca, Nevada Base. The technicians began their work of creating a virtual computer-generated image, a version of Luis Angel Alveraz.

The computer-generated image was much like the process which put the deceased Paul Walker back into his car in the Fast and Furious 7 movie. The same imaging process when Dwayne Johnson, The Rock, was transformed into an overweight, high school kid in Central Intelligence.

Although similar, the Nevada Base GCI version of Luis Alveraz was more life-like than any movie studio could create. All this was completed before the barber cut his bushy, black hair before he shaved before removing his semi-permanent brown contacts.

The handlers gave Dale a script to read as if he were giving words to an animated cartoon. However, these words would be to create real-life scenarios to save Dale's life. The new mission would be Dale without all the hair, always shaven and with his natural sky-blue eyes.

Dale had to change so he could never be in the position of being identified by anyone from his last mission. When he arrived in North Carolina, he would be another man with another past.

Luis Angel Alveraz had to die a believable death so no one would be looking for him. Dale's face would be different only because of his haircut, shave, and natural blue eyes. His accent and dialect would be as if he had come from Ontario, Canada, with a Frenchman's cadence.

Dale was at the Yucca, Nevada Base two days before his 'death' was arranged. He watched the recording of an argument with a drug mule, a recording of a meeting with a cartel submarine builder, and a romp with a cartel lieutenant's girlfriend.

They appeared to be so real the drug mule, the sub builder, the lieutenant, and even the girl would believe it was somehow true. There were also pictures of him in restaurants, boat docks, and talking to other people on dates before his death.

However, the last video he watched made cold chills run along his arms, causing chills to run down his spine. The footage showed him on his go-fast-boat a few miles off the shore of Columbia in shark-infested waters.

As he watched, what appeared to be Luis Angle Alveraz, was blown up in a fireball sending parts of him into shark-infested water. The sharks went into a feeding frenzy as the boat pieces sank or floated away.

Technological geniuses provided a Columbian cartel member to show proof. The fictitious dark skin man recorded the event from a nearby yacht. The video soon to be shared on social media. The genius of edited made Angel go away forever.

It took a few minutes for Dale to collect himself after he watched the whole video. When the Federation agent told him the distribution of information distributed on social media and fake news reports, he felt relief.

No one would be looking for who he was. It was now time to be someone else, and he had two more years of his mission to complete. He was glad his next two-year mission would soon be over, and most of all, he wished the death of Rex had also been a computer-generated image.

Dale kept running the scenario thru his mind remembering the moments Rex signed his death warrant. A cartel member caught having sex with a well know dealer's, main woman. On the day of the attack, he and Rex had fought hard with the hired gunman and his team members.

Dale was knocked out and stabilized with zip ties. He woke as someone poured cold beer on his face. Terrified, he watched Rex's beating and the gunshots entering his knees and his groin. They beheaded him, and lastly, the cartel member put Rex into a cage of crocodiles: they quickly made his body parts disappear.

The cartel member cut his ties as the gunman said, "Let this be a lesson to you. Go before I change my mind." He had hobbled off the best he could, knowing there was nothing else he could do.

EPISODE 2

Dale lay beside a road in Blackstone County, North Carolina, listening to the people around him. He heard a female voice, male voices, and what he believed were the voices of children.

Dale had been lying beside the road since before the morning light waiting for someone to discover him. Now he was waiting for the moment to come out of his simulated unconsciousness. He had to time it just right.

As he lay on the side of the road with his eyes closed, he thought about how he felt. He felt nervous, almost terrified. Since he was born, he received training for this situation, so these emotions surprised him.

He listened while he tried to control his breathing and heart rate, remembering he needed to use a different language and accent, English with a French Canadian accent.

A male voice said, "The ambulance should be here any minute."

Dale felt a touch. The person checking his pulse said, "E. H., his pulse feels normal." He felt the touch move near his head wound where he had smashed his head with a rock.

The woman said, "This injury doesn't seem to be deep, but it looks like he may need some stitches. Best if he has an x-ray to be sure he doesn't have a concussion."

Dale moaned and reached his hand towards his head. What sounded like a young man said, "Don't move. We will get you checked out as soon as we can. Where do you hurt?"

Dale opened his eyes and saw the voice came from a man about his age. His pulse rate increased as the young man said, "Do you know what happened to you?"

"Daddy, what is wrong with him? Is he going to die? Are you gonna' fix him? What's his name?" A child said.

Looking past the young man, he saw a male child asking questions so quickly there was no time to answer. He also saw a younger female child clinging to the leg of an older, gray-haired man.

Dale sat up. The adult female was telling him it would be best if he lay still until the ambulance came.

He faked his voice as if he were trying to speak. His voice quivered as he said, "I'm fine. I will be fine." Dale moaned as he reached for his hat. He sighed as he tried to get up.

He looked at the older man standing near and said, "Help me stand up."

As the older man reached for Dale, the younger man said, "You should wait until the paramedics get here.

The older man ignored the younger man as he reached for Dale's arm.

Dale was surprised at the strength and the gentleness of the man. After he steadied himself, he put on his western hat and reached out to shake the man's hand. Dale investigated the old man's calm face and said, "Hello, I'm Dale Weaver."

"I'm E. H. Denton, and this is my son, Larry. He pointed and said, this is my daughter-in-law, Katherine, and added, "These are my two grandchildren, Jordan and Skylar.

Dale smiled reached to give Larry a firm handshake. He gently shook Katherine's hand, and then he shook Jordan's hand with a funny pumping action. Quickly he sized up the little girl, took off his hat, and made a sweeping bow.

Skylar smiled and looked up at her mother, "Mama, he must be a prince. Only a prince would bow to a princess, and you always say I am a princess."

As Dale placed his hat back on his head, Jordan said, "Don't be silly, Skylar. He is not a prince. A prince doesn't wear a cowboy hat and boots."

E. H., Larry, and Katherine were still laughing as the ambulance arrived. Larry walked over to the two paramedics and explained how they found Dale lying beside the road with a head wound.

The three men walked toward Dale as he let the paramedics take his arm on each side and walked him to the ambulance. He sat on the back of the ambulance as they examined his head. Dwight Gacy cleaned the wound as Stanley Hall watched. Dwight said, "They can repair this as soon as we get you to the emergency room."

Dale spoke firmly but still with a nervous tremor, "No, I'm not going. It will be fine."

Katherine walked over, looked closer as she said, "Dwight, press it together, put on the liquid stitch, and add tape. It will be better than nothing."

While Dwight was tending to Dale, he asked, "What happened to you?"

Remembering his training, Dale became calmer and answered with his Canadian accent, "I got a ride from two men heading to Raleigh. They drove me here and made me get out of the car. The last thing I remember was something hitting my head. He stood and reached his right hand to his jeans pocket and said, "They must have gotten my wallet."

"What was in it?" asked E. H.

He looked at the five adults and two children who were staring at him and said, "Only twenty dollars."

He took off his left boot. They watched as a grin showing a perfect set of white teeth crossed his face. He removed his sock, reached into it, and pulled out a plastic bag containing his driver's license and a small roll of money.

"I try to prepare," he said as he thought about the thousands of dollars hidden in the soles of his boots, emergency money he would use to establish himself in the communities of Blackstone County.

Everyone laughed. Dale turned to the two ambulance workers, reached out for a handshake as a Caucasian man said, "I'm Dwight Gacy, and this young pup is Stanley Hall."

"I am Dale Weaver. Nice to meet you," Dale replied.

Dwight said, "Man, you really should go get checked out. After you get checked out, we will find you a ride to Raleigh."

"No. I will be fine. I just need food. Will you be driving by a restaurant?"

"Edward's Diner is right outside of Stonehope," said Dwight. "We can go there. I wouldn't mind having a bit of food myself. They serve a mighty fine breakfast," and then added, "do you want breakfast, Stanley?"

"Y-y-y-yeah. I'm starved."

"You are always starved," said Dwight as he winked at Katherine.

Stanley bowed his head and shuffled his feet nervously before heading for the passenger side of the ambulance.

Dale turned back to the family who saved him. "Thank you for helping me. It was nice to meet you. I wish I could find some way to repay you for your kindness."

Katherine smiled and said, "Just take care of yourself and, next time, find a better way of transportation."

"I will do that. I guess picking up a ride can be dangerous." Again, Dale reached out and shook Jordan's hand and said, "Thank you, partner." Then he again removed his hat and made another sweeping bow to Skylar as he said, "You are the most beautiful princess I have ever met. I hope we meet again once upon a time."

"See! I told you he was a prince because he said once upon a time. Only a prince would say those words." Skylar wrinkled her nose and made a face at her brother, saying, "Boys don't know anything. Anybody can see he is a cowboy prince who lost his horse."

"Dale managed not to laugh at the little girl and said, "My horse is at my home in Canada. I will have him brought to me one day. Then I will bring him to see you. His name is Magic." Skylar's eyes widened.

Dwight was shifting from one foot to the other as he said, "Dale, we need to be moving on if we are going to get some breakfast."

After tipping his hat to the three adults, Dale turned to Dwight; while still in character, he said, "Let's ride."

EPISODE 3

When the ambulance arrived at Edward's Diner, Stanley and Dale entered laughing at a joke Dwight told. They went inside, still smiling. Dale and Stanley followed Dwight to a table near a window. A waitress was at the table before they were seated. Dale removed his hat and placed it on an empty chair as he looked at the name tag on the waitress's uniform. His smile widened as he said, "Bonjour, Pam."

Pam Mann looked at Dwight and asked, "Who is your friendly French cowboy?"

"His name is Dale Weaver. We found him near the Denton place. Someone bashed his head for twenty dollars."

Pam looked at the bandage on his forehead and said, "Ouch. Where are you from, Dale?"

"Canada," said Dale knowing his I.D. and his personal history had been changed and placed on the internet in every conceivable way.

Dwight constantly drilled Dale on his new documentation during his transport, the place he supposedly was born and raised, and Dale's pretend family. He had rehearsed it so many times he almost believed it himself.

"Man of many words?" she asked.

Dwight spoke up. "Don't be so nosey, Pam."

Pam looked at Dwight and sarcastically said, "Sorry. What would Y'all like to order?"

Stanley wouldn't look Pam in the eyes. Dwight knew how this went, so he said, "Stanley and I want two eggs over easy, country ham, grits, fried apples, and two biscuits. I like black coffee, and Stanley wants a cup with half coffee and half milk. That's it.

Pam looked at Dale. "And you?"

"I'll have what Dwight ordered plus a glass of orange juice."

After Pam left the table, Dwight sarcastically asked, "So you speak Spanish?"

Dale tried very hard not to be as sarcastic as Dwight and answered with a perfect Canadian-French accent, "Je ne parle pas Espagnol. Je parle Francais."

Dale noticed the smile Stanley tried to hide and the pleasure he received when he told Dwight, "He'he sp-speaks French."

Dwight looked at Stanley with contempt and said, "He needs to speak English. He's in the United States!"

Looking directly into Dwight's eyes, Dale said apologetically, "Sorry. French is a second language to me. I will try to be more careful."

How long have you been in the States?" Dwight asked.

Dale thought, *Here I go. Don't make a mistake.* Remembering the information on his new passport, he said, "I was born in the United States. We moved to Canada three months after I was born. My father was from Canada. He met my mother while he was on a trip to purchase a boat in Michigan. They fell in love, but she did not want to move to Canada.

Neither one of them knew my mother was pregnant when he left. After I was born, my Mother's father got in touch with my father. My father immediately went to Michigan to get my mother and me. They were married in Canada. I have dual citizenship."

"So, how come you don't speak Canadian?" Dwight asked Dale with his same sarcasm.

Dale looked at Dwight. He did not want to insult one of the first people he met, so he said, "My father was born in France, so I learned two languages when I was growing up."

My mother died when I was ten. She and I had flown to the United States to visit my grandparents. When it was time to return, they agreed to drive us back so they could visit Thunder Bay. When my grandparents, mother, and I were on the way back to Canada, there was a horrific automobile accident. I was thrown clear. The car burst into flames, making me the only one to survive.

"Th-th-that's sad, said Stanley. It's a g-g-good thing your f-f-father d-d-didn't go." Even though he was speaking, Stanley was still thinking, is this THE Dale Weaver?

Pam walked up with a tray. "Excuse me, Cowboy." She placed the coffees and Dale's juice on the table and said, "I'll be right back with your breakfast."

"Je vous remercie, Pam," Dale said as he pretended not to see the sneer on Dwight's face.

Dale took a swallow of his juice and continued with the story. "As I was saying, my father emigrated from Paris to Canada when he was fourteen with his older brother, Lucien. They went to Nunavut, Canada, where both found a job working for a company mining for gold."

Pam walked up and said, "Sorry it is taking so long. As you can see, it is a busier than usual morning. Everyone remained quiet until she walked away.

After a bit, Stanley fidgeted with his fork and asked Dale if he would finish his story. Dale drank a bit of his coffee and began.

"Five years after my father and my uncle arrived in Nunavut; Uncle Lucien was knifed to death in a bar fight. Since my father hated working in the mines and the artic weather, he took the money he and his brother had saved and left for Thunder Bay, Ontario."

"My father and Uncle Lucien had heard about the warmer climate and the great fishing. They had been planning to go to the Thunder Bay area as soon as they saved enough money."

Dwight stopped slurping his coffee and asked, "What was the bar fight about?"

Stanley looked at Dwight like he was an idiot, but he didn't say anything.

Dale drank more coffee and said, "It was over a woman."

Dwight smiled. Dale had said something which he could relate, "Was she good lookin'?"

"Yes, she was a stunning French woman. However, my Father said she was after Uncle Lucien's money. They had saved a good part of what they made in the mines."

"Sounds like she was smart too. Beauty and smarts will get a woman a long way if she plays it right." Dwight interjected and asked, "Dale, why did you come through Blackstone County?"

Pam walked up with the food and placed it on the table. Stanley and Dale said, "Thank you."

"My Papa told me we had no other family in the United States or Canada. So, after my father died three months ago, I had no family left. I decided to take a tour of the United States. I began the trip from Thunder Bay and first went to Maine as I wanted to work my way down the Atlantic Coast." Dale thought, *I probably gave too much information.*

Stanley spoke, "You are aw-w-ways from the coast."

"I was in a Wilmington, North Carolina bar, and someone was talking about Raleigh and how nice it was. I decided to see what they were talking about." Dale knew he was back on script and said, "I have plenty of time to take side trips, so I picked up a ride to Raleigh."

He looked at Stanley and said, "What do you think of Raleigh, Stanley?"

Stanley looked surprised. He was not used to people asking him questions. Without hesitation, he said, "Th-th-there is a l-l-lot to do in R-r-Raleigh. You c-c-can go to museums, w-w-walk areas which have homes o-o-over a hundred years old or go to some great restaurants."

"The c-c-capital building was c-c-completed in 1840. It is in the Greek revival st-st-style of architecture and is a National Historic Landmark. Downtown R-r-Raleigh has reinvented itself. Since s-s-shoppers mainly had gone to surrounding shopping centers, the downtown area began to die. P-p-people with a vision are n-n-now using some of the old b-b-b-buildings to create apartments, cond-d-dominiums, and new locally owned sm-sm-all b-b-businesses.

There are all k-k-kinds of nightlife in Raleigh. My f-f-favorite is the Water Trough Saloon. It has all kinds of music such as Country, Rock, Top 40 and R&B. The d-d-d-ance floors are great. Garth Brooks was there before he became r-r-really famous."

Pam walked up while Stanley was talking. Suddenly Stanley stopped talking and looked at Dwight and then at Pam. Both mouths were open in disbelief. Still in shock, Pam refilled the coffee cups without saying a word before she walked away.

Dale felt uneasy for Stanley and wondered if he was indeed his contact. He guessed Stanley did not usually talk, and Dale had never heard anyone stutter

He looked at Stanley even though Stanley had lowered his eyes towards his plate. "Thanks, Stanley. Maybe you could accompany me to Raleigh and show me the places you mentioned."

Stanley did not look up and only said, "S-s-sure."

Dwight was still looking at Stanley, looking at him as if he were a stranger. He had always thought Stanley was slow-minded. Even though Stanley went to the community college to be a paramedic, he felt the teachers passed him out of pity.

Stanley was the only black person on the rescue squad, and Dwight never asked him to help with patients unless it was a simple duty.

What he did not know was Stanley had an IQ of 180 and a photographic memory. He had graduated from his classes with a 4.3-grade average. Stanley stuttered and was shy, not dumb.

The three men began to eat again without speaking. Dale ate slowly. He was enjoying the taste of the food except for the white stuff Dwight called grits.

Dale watched Dwight and Stanley noticing how they ate their food. He hoped others in the restaurant could not tell this was the first time he had eaten a Southern breakfast.

When Dwight finished his food, he began nursing his cup of coffee. He asked Dale, "What do you do for a living, Dale?

Dale was cupping his hands around his coffee cup and trying not to let the others know he hated coffee. He sipped it and then answered, "My father was a fisherman, but his hobby was working on automobiles. He taught me. We mostly worked on older cars; automobiles built before 1960."

Dwight said, "Why older cars?"

"I do not know if there was a reason Father liked to work on older cars. Sometimes he would restore an older model and sell it. Living as we did and where we did, we didn't need much cash. We caught fish and hunted for meat. We purchased other things like beans and rice at the local trapping supply store. It was a good life." Dale was looking at Dwight and was thinking, and I wish Rex were here. I know he would have something to say about these grits.

Stanley broke his silence, "D-d-dale, Rodney Medlin is looking for a me-me-mechanic if you w-w-would like to stay in Stonehope for a w-w-while." As soon as he felt Dwight eyeing him again, he looked down at his plate.

Dwight looked at Stanley, thinking, how does he know about Rodney having a job opening?

"Yes. I believe I would be interested. Where is Rodney's business?"

This time Stanley looked up and into Dale's eyes as he said without stuttering, "It's on Branch Street behind his house. He also has an apartment over the garage. He needs the rent money if you need somewhere to stay."

While Dwight was again staring at Stanley as his radio beeped, he pressed the button to answer. After hearing the location, he said, "Got to go, Stanley," He stood up and put enough money on the table for the three meals and a tip. Dwight said, "OK smart boy, let's get going."

Dale barely had time to thank them before Dwight and Stanley were out of the door. He motioned for Pam to come over. When she arrived, he said, "Dwight left this money. Is it enough?"

"Yes, Cowboy. It is more than enough. You make sure you bring those dreamy, blue eyes back in here. I'll be glad to serve you."

Dale felt his face flush. Now, this is new, he said to himself and thought, *Rex was one man who got the ladies flirtation.* Recovering quickly, he asked, "Can you tell me the way to Branch Street." He left the restaurant on foot.

Later in the evening, Dale sat at a tiny dining table with a burger and fries from Simon's Food Bar, only two blocks away from his new garage apartment. Dale was thinking of all the events of the day.

The person who stuck in his mind most was Katherine; she was a beauty, and when he shook her hand, there seemed to be a pulse of electricity. When the thought entered his mind, he reminded himself Katherine was married and felt shame.

As Dale sat at the small table, he decided he was pleased with the day. He had just arrived, and he had a job, a small apartment, and a friend.

He was anxious to begin this part of his mission; he could go home in just two more years. Now he had found Stanley; he knew he must get more serious about Blackstone County's mission. Brutus would be going down.

EPISODE 4

Stanley sat in his tiny house on Canon Street. He lived in Stonehope all his life and was born at home, the same place he was living. He lived in colored town. It was what older white people called the area where blacks had lived for decades.

He never knew his father. His grandma told Stanley his father was no good and left as soon as he discovered his mother was pregnant. He and his mother lived with his grandma and grandpa from that time forward.

Stanley's mother started doing drugs when he was in the second grade. She would sometimes be gone for weeks but would always come back home to dry out and make promises she never kept. When she came home, he was eleven years old; she came home in a cheap, wooden coffin.

His grandpa was a WWII veteran and gravely injured in the war. Stanley's grandfather believed in the Bible and sometimes thought the belt was a necessary tool for raising children. However, Stanley only received his grandfather's belt once; he told him a lie about breaking a dish.

When Stanley was thirteen, his grandfather died. Even though he had veteran benefits, he had lung cancer and did not go to the doctor.

He attributed all his symptoms to old age, and when he began to have breathing problems, he went to the doctor. It was too late, and he died six weeks later.

His grandma clean houses three days a week until she was diagnosed with breast cancer. People in colored town didn't go to doctors very often, especially the older generation. Even though Stanley's grandmother saw what happened to her husband, she still refused to go to a doctor.

When she finally went, it was too late. She died two days after Stanley's eighteenth birthday. His grandmother left him the house and the tiny plot of land it was on. He felt blessed for having had his grandparents, the land, and a home.

Stanley sat at the kitchen table with his laptop. He had a crockpot going which contained a ham hock and some black-eyed peas. His grandma also had left him an insurance policy. He had used most of it to put in a heat and air unit and a new roof, and he put the remainder of the money into a savings account.

As he browsed through a website about paramedics, he thought of all the things which lead him to this place, time, and circumstances. He made excellent grades in grade school and high school, but no one noticed except for Ms. Tetterton.

He was the small black boy who stuttered. He was bullied and learned early on to keep his emotions to himself. He used his slight frame and stuttering to make jokes and do other things, making the other students laugh. When he graduated, he received the class clown accolade instead of most likely to succeed.

Two days after his graduation Ms. Tetterton came to see him at his home. He was surprised but pleased she came. She brought him a book of jokes and a box of her homemade carrot-cake muffins.

After he thanked her, she asked if she could visit for a few minutes. He quickly agreed but had no idea the visit would lead him to be involved in taking down a drug cartel one day.

They sat across from each other at the kitchen table with iced tea and muffins. Stanley would never forget how she skipped from one thing to the other as she talked to him. She told him it took "a lot of smarts" to be funny. She mentioned several old-time comedians like Red Skeleton, Robin Williams, Carol Burnett, and Tim Conway.

She told him sometimes; he would need to be quiet because he could learn more than anyone in the room. She had said, "Stanley, don't let anyone hold you back and don't stop learning; not at any age. Read as much as you can and decide what is essential; with a computer available, you have no limit.

Later, Stanley would remember her saying, "At some point in your life, you will use all the knowledge you have gained. Learn another language, maybe two or three. You are smart enough to do anything you want to do."

Ms. Tetterton had continued the conversation by saying, "Stanley, you have been my favorite student of all my teaching years. I have recommended you for a particular job. You will be contacted soon."

He remembered her getting up from the table and giving him a big bear hug. Before she left, she had held him at arm's length and smiled as she said, "I am blessed to have you as my student, Stanley." Later he found out she left Blackstone County to teach elsewhere. He never expected to see or hear from her again.

There were a few of his classmates who lived in the town of Stonehope. Most had gone to college, but even those who did not continue their education found jobs in other cities and states. He rarely saw anyone from his grammar and high school days.

It didn't bother him except for one person, Sunny Tupelo. He had a crush on her longer than he could remember. He often pulled up the memories of her being nice to him in school.

She was the only classmate who never made fun of him. She even asked him to the Senior Dance. Sunny wore flat shoes instead of heels the night of the dance, a gesture not lost on Stanley. During the dance, she had told him that they would forever be best friends right before she kissed him.

Now she was a famous actress. Even so, she would occasionally send him a handwritten note about where she was and what she was doing. She gave him an address so he could send her mail. Sometimes he sent a message, a birthday card, a Christmas card, or sometimes a letter about what was going on in his life. She always acknowledged his mail with a thank you note and a short message.

Sunny was the only classmate who knew about his extraordinary intelligence, which is what she called it. She was also the only person in the area who knew about his real job, not his career as a paramedic. Every time she wrote him concerning the job, he burned the letter. He didn't want to, but he had to for her sake and his.

With those thoughts, Stanley logged off his computer, went for a beer, looked upward, and said, "Sorry, Grandma. I won't ever drink too many." It was his way of respecting his grandmother and how she had raised him.

Stanley sat on the recliner he purchased a few days after he got the job as a paramedic. He picked up the remote and searched for something to watch on TV. It was the first Saturday in weeks. He couldn't find anything he wanted to watch, so he sat in silence, drinking his beer.

When he finished, he tried to think of something to do. He didn't have any hobbies except fishing, and it was too hot and humid to go fishing.

As he mindlessly looked at the TV screen, an advertisement came on with a western theme which made him think of the man Pam called Cowboy.

He turned the television off, grabbed his car keys, and headed to the garage where Dale worked. He felt comfortable around him because he talked to him like a real person, not a black man who stuttered. But then, Dale knew who he was, and Stanley hoped he was here to   help   take   down   Brutus.

EPISODE 5

When Larry left his job as a fireman, the morning temperature was already seventy-eight degrees. He arrived home, walked onto the back porch, and opened the back-screen door. When the hinge made a squeaking sound, his father's dog, Ratchet, came onto the porch. Larry bent down, patted his head, and said, "Hey, old boy. How are you doing this hot day?" He pulled the door further open and reminded himself to oil the hinges later in the day.

It was a little past six. Larry hoped he could sneak in and have some time with his wife before she had to leave for the hospital. He closed the door as he entered the kitchen, went to the hall, and slowly went up the stairs as each step made its own sound.

He smiled at the memory of all the Christmas mornings he had crept down the stairs only to find his mother standing at the bottom. She would immediately send him back to bed. When he was little, he couldn't understand how she knew.

When he became a teenager, he tried to find a quiet spot on each stair step. He never did find a quiet spot on any of them and thought the noises had to be a conspiracy concocted by his parents.

His dad, E. H., had often told him, "Son, you don't know what strict is." It always was the response after he had complained his father and mother never let him do the things the other kids did. He thought *it's funny how things come full circle because I tell my children the same thing.*

He was home from work after a four-day shift at the Blackstone County Fire Department, and he knew Katherine was going in at eight o'clock for a twelve-hour shift.

When he reached the top of the stairs, he heard the shower. He went into the bedroom, stripped, and quietly went to the bathroom. He slowly opened the shower curtains as he whispered his wife's name. She pulled back the curtain and smiled.

He stepped into the enclosed tub and wrapped his arms around his wife as he kissed her softly. Soon the kiss became passionate. Someone hit the soap bar, and it fell to the floor of the tub. Larry slipped and fell to his knees. They both started giggling as Katherine reached for Larry's hand to help him up.

When they left the shower, they walked towards the bed, leaving wet footprints behind them. There they continued to make love. When they finished, they just looked at each other and laughed. It was what they always did; neither knew why but it happened every time.

Katherine hopped up and finished getting ready for her nursing shift. Larry said, "I'll go make you some breakfast."

"Thanks, Honey, but I won't have time to eat."

"I'm sorry," said Larry.

Quickly Katherine replied, "I'm not. We needed the time together." She added, "Don't forget tomorrow is Jordan's birthday. When I get a break, I'll call, and we will talk about the plans."

As she picked up her purse, Larry rushed to her. He put his right hand on her cheek and just looked at her. Then he kissed her on her forehead and laughed. "Go, my sexy wife, I love you!"

When Katherine went downstairs, the children ran to kiss her. E. H. was making breakfast and turned to her and said what he always said, "Have a blessed day, Sweetheart," and added, "I love what you do for this family."

Katherine Denton left the house feeling like the luckiest woman in the world.

EPISODE 6

E. H. Denton pulled into the driveway. It had been a quiet trip back from church. When he stopped the car, he looked towards Larry and said, Son, it's a beautiful day. Why don't we take the kids fishing after lunch?

Before Larry could answer, Jordon was saying, "Yaa, I'm going fishing."

Skylar began whining and said, "Why can't I go fishing? I want to go fishing too.

E. H. got out of the car and headed to the back porch while Larry was trying to explain to Skylar that they were going fishing but had to eat their lunch first.

Skylar looked at her dad and smiled at him, and then she aimed a smirk at Jordan, saying, "Daddy is taking me fishing too."

Larry saw the smirk and wondered where she had learned it. When they all were inside E. H. said, "Y'all change your clothes and come back down. I cooked a pot roast in the crock pot, and we'll have some heated rolls.

Go along, kids. First one down gets the first buttered roll." The two rushed out of the room, arguing about who would be first. Larry looked at his dad, shrugged his shoulders, and smiled.

The kitchen was peaceful, but E. H. knew it would not be for long. He began thinking the same thing he had been thinking about for months. Sunday was the worst day without his wife, Sadie. She was the one who always prepared the table for lunch after church.

Sometimes he felt he could bear the pain no longer. He missed his wife every moment of every day. He missed her because he always used the Sunday tablecloth, napkins, and the china they purchased to celebrate their first wedding anniversary.

When he touched a plate, a memory would flash into his mind. Sometimes he smiled, and sometimes he would feel tears leak from his eyes. He always set the table for the six of them. Today there would be two empty seats and two unused place settings; Katherine's setting and Sadie's setting.

Larry walked in. He saw E. H.'s face and recognized the pain in his father's eyes. Larry missed his mother too. His pain was still sharp, but he had Katherine and the kids. They helped him cope. It seemed his father had the worst time on Sundays before and after church.

All his parent's friends continued to talk to E. H. and tried to treat him the same, but most of their friends were couples, and the conversations were shorter and sometimes strained. The couples didn't realize they treated E. H. differently, but E. H. did.

The kids came through the door. Jordan pushed the door so hard it slammed against the wall. With the loud noise came a stern look from Larry.

"Sorry, Daddy, I didn't mean to push it so hard," said Jordan.

"Daddy, he didn't mean it. We are so hungry. Please don't be mad at Jordan," Skylar begged.

Before Larry could speak, Jordan grabbed Skylar and hugged Skylar while saying, "You're the best sister ever."

E. H. and Larry broke out in laughter. The spirits in the Denton household were lifted.

EPISODE 7

Junior Maddox pulled into the driveway of the old, brick, ranch-style home. The grass needed mowing, and there were several newspapers on the front porch. He pulled his Jaguar beside his father's patrol car. A skinny cat ran from the porch as Junior walked up the steps. He looked in the window. His father was sitting at the red-topped kitchen table, a relic from the 1950s. He was cleaning his service pistol. Junior knocked on the door and then opened it as his father, Vernon Maddox, reached for his other gun in his military-style boot.

"Damn, Son. Ain't you got a bit of sense? One of the days I'm gonna shoot you," slurred Vernon.

Junior paid him no mind. He removed his expensive suit jacket and rolled up his sleeves. "It's hot in here. Why don't you have on the air conditioner?"

Vernon grunted and continued to clean his revolver.

Opening the refrigerator, Junior asked, "What do you eat? There is nothing in here but some molded cheese and cheap beer." He slammed the frig door and opened a cabinet door.

He saw six bottles of Jack Daniels and two bottles of Smirnoff vodka. He slammed the cabinet door and turned as he glared at his father.

Without looking up, Vernon said, "What the hell did you come home for?"

Junior shook his head, turned, and put his hand on the doorknob. He turned back to his father and said, "I'm going to the diner and get some food. What do you want?"

"It doesn't matter to me. Just don't slam another damn bitchin' door."

When Junior returned, Vernon had reassembled his service pistol and returned it to the holster; the holster and gun lay on the table. The air condition was running, and the room was cooler.

There were two unopened beers on the table. Vernon was staring mindlessly at the calendar on the wall; January with snow-covered mountains.

Junior came home with two of everything. He set a covered plate and a plastic container with apple pie in front of his father and the same on the opposite side of the table.

He opened another bag and pulled out two large cups of iced tea, one for him and one for Vernon.

When Vernon opened the plate and saw the chicken pastry, collards, and lima beans, Junior thought he saw a smile. He tried to choose his father's favorites. They both ate in silence. Vernon even drank the tea before he opened his beer.

When Vernon finished eating, he straightened in his chair and belched. Junior turned his head so his father wouldn't see him smile. It was the closest thing to a thank you Junior would hear from his father.

Junior said, "There is a new man in town; he showed up in front of the Denton place.

Vernon got up and went to the refrigerator, and got another beer. He sat down and said, "They found him in front of their yard with a gash on his head. Said some guys picked him up, drove him out of town, and robbed him."

"Where did he come from? Junior asked.

"Don't know. He said from Canada. He went to work at Rodney Medlin's garage. I heard he was good on old cars."

"What's his name?

"Dale Weaver; been trying to get him checked out but can't find much. He's got a Canadian driver's license. Got the little nigger, Stanley, trying to get more information on the internet? He says everything he finds looks legit and says the Weaver fellow don't talk much."

Junior asked, "Why aren't you checking him out yourself?"

"Damn, Junior, you are the one who went to a fancy lawyer college? I don't know anything about computers. Why do you want to check out every new person who shows up in Blackstone County? Damn it! People move from one place to the other; it happens."

"Nobody moves to Stonehope." Junior started with a normal voice and then began to yell and waved his arms around.

"When a man has no past to be found, you worry. Dammit, Vernon, you worry. You check him out. If you suspect him of being undercover, then you do away with him."

"You know how it works. You know, goddamn it. You know. What the hell is wrong with you? You need to dig a hole in the woods for him. You know what I did with the last creep. I can't take chances on him being undercover."

As Junior glared at the old man, he thought how he had taken Vernon's old marijuana business from the '70s and turned it into something powerful and profitable. He was known in the illegal drug community as the Gold Dust Drug Czar and, locally, as Brutus.

Junior Maddox controlled the travel of drugs up and down the I-95 from the northern states to the southern borders of North Carolina. Also, east of Raleigh to the Atlantic Ocean. He was making millions and did anything needed to keep his enterprise going.

Vernon did not respond to Junior as he cleaned the table. He took the trash out to the bin and then put his unopened beer back into the refrigerator. Vernon knew any response he made would be the wrong one.

He then looked at Junior with raised eyebrows, sat down, and poured himself a tea glass of Jack Daniels. He sat quietly nursing it while wondering what he had done to create a ruthless murderer.

He never dreamed when he let Junior into his lucrative pot business; he would take it to a whole new level. He was afraid for his son and had been out of the drug business since his son graduated from high school and demanded to take over.

Junior sat down opposite Vernon, hoping to start a normal conversation. "Heard you hired a local guy at the department; how is he doing?"

Vernon looked at Junior like he did when he was a small boy wondering what had happened. He felt shame and disappointment. Why was Junior so callous? He sometimes found it hard to believe the cold-blooded things his son did.

He knew if Junior were not his son, he would have taken him down long ago. He felt culpable for the atrocious things his son did but couldn't find it within himself to stop him. Vernon also knew that if he crossed Junior, he wouldn't hesitate to get rid of his father.

While Vernon felt guilty, Junior saw the look on his father's face as disgust and hatred. He always felt Vernon did not want him. Junior had never received a hug or any word of encouragement from his father. He felt like a ghost in the house.

His mother had died at childbirth, and his aunt, Vernon's sister, Agnes, moved in with them. She raised him as if he was a burden she had to bear. As soon as Junior went away to college, she moved out of the house.

When Vernon saw the pain in his son's eyes, he tipped the glass up and drank it all. He wanted to forget all the things running through his mind, and the only way he knew to forget was with Jack.

What he wanted was for his son to have a normal life. Vernon brushed the whisky from his lips and thought, *my son is a ruthless, powerful drug kingpin.*

When Vernon finished the first glass of Jack, he poured four fingers more and gulped it down. He got up and walked into the bathroom without turning to look back at Junior. He didn't want to contemplate the inevitable fate of his son.

When Vernon Maddox walked away, Junior looked at the back of his father. In Junior's mind, his father turning his back and walking away was another rejection.

He rose, pushed his chair under the table, walked out of the kitchen and into the dark living room. He walked to the window and opened the blinds.

Junior turned on the television and sat on the sofa. He changed the channels until he found an old movie. He was thankful he had cable TV put in, although he knew his father never watched TV. Vernon went to work, returned home, got drunk, slept, and got up and went to work again.

Junior rarely came home. It was no use. He and his father would never get along. He sat watching the television until he heard his father stumble from the bathroom to his bedroom. He heard the old bed springs as his father fell upon the bed. Sheriff Vernon Maddox immediately began to snore.

Junior rose from the sofa, turned the television off, and placed the remote on the old, boot-scratched coffee table. He walked out of the old house and headed back to his condo in Raleigh. He wondered why he bothered to come to see his father. Suddenly, a new seed of doubt interred his thoughts; Junior wondered if he could trust Vernon.

EPISODE 8

When the alarm clock sounded, Dale sat up, swung his legs over the edge of the bed, stretched his arms high, and took a deep breath.

He began his daily routine as he showered quickly, put his clothes on, and went to Rex's room. Rex and the woman beside him were snoring. All the covers were on the floor, and both people were au naturel.

Dale yelled, "Get up, Rex." Neither of the naked people moved, so Dale raised his voice and barked his order, "Get up, dammit!"

Rex opened his eyes and angrily said, "Get out of here."

"No. Not until you get up," said Dale. Rex turned over on his side away from the woman."

Dale walked out of the room and went to the refrigerator. He took out a gallon jug of water, took the lid off, turned it up, and gulped a couple of swallows as he thought, *I believe this is cold enough.*

He carried the jug to Rex's bedroom, stood beside the bed, and poured cold water up and down the length of Rex's body. Rex quickly stood up beside the bed and took a swing at Dale.

Dale expected the action, so he jumped back and then bent double, laughing. Rex was cursing in Spanish, and Dale laughed harder. He quickly went to the other side of the bed and poured cold water on the woman. She sat up quickly and was swearing even more than Rex.

Dale demanded, "Rex, get your ass in the shower. You know we have a trip today."

Dale then turned his attention to the woman as she was pulling up her cut-off jeans. He reached for her blouse and threw it at the brown girl shouting, "Get out of here now and don't steal anything."

The dark-skinned woman slung her long black hair away from her face and yelled, "Eres un culo de cabras." With her shirt and sandals in her hand, she headed for the front door bare-breasted. She turned around long enough to spit towards Dale.

Dale went to the door behind her and yelled, "I might be a goat's ass, but you are just a whore with a dirty mouth."

Dale woke up and looked around his room. He looked at the clock. It was one o'clock, but it was not dark. When he realized it was the afternoon, he jumped out of bed and stood dazed.

He looked around for Rex. His tiny apartment was unfamiliar, and he couldn't remember where he was. He sat down on the edge of the bed and put his head in his hands. Slowly his new life came back to him.

Dale looked at the calendar on the wall. There was a picture of a shapely blond sitting provocatively on the hood of a red 1970 Chevelle SS. Confused, and Dale stared at the calendar a moment before he remembered what day it was.

He had started to work on the Bel Air at five-thirty Saturday afternoon. He worked without thinking about time. Once he stopped working, he cleaned the garage and went to his apartment. When he took a shower, it was three-fifteen Sunday morning. He had been hungry, but he was too tired to eat, so he drank a glass of milk

After Dale realized he had been dreaming, he walked towards the back window of his apartment and stood. His head was clearing, but the anger he felt with Rex lingered.

He went to the bathroom, splashed cold water on his face, and then shaved. The next thought was food. He decided to call Stanley and see if he wanted to go to Edwards Diner.

Dale and Stanley were on their way to the diner. Because Stanley was on call, they were driving in separate vehicles. When they arrived, they both walked into Edwards Diner and found a booth. Stanley laid his radio on the table and said, "It's been sl-sl-slow today. I hope it st-st-stays that w-w-way."

While Dale was putting his hat on a vacant chair, Pam rushed to the table. "Hello, Cowboy," she said in her sexiest voice. What do you two want today? The Sunday special is fried pork chops, string bean casserole, creamed potatoes, and homemade yeast rolls.

Before Dale could answer, Stanley said, "I'll have the special with sweet iced tea, and what desserts do you have today? And, Pam, will you also put the food on a take-out plate since I'm on duty?

Pam was not used to Stanley speaking up. Usually, he came with Dwight, and he let Dwight order for him. What surprised her more than him speaking up was Stanley did not stutter.

She said, "Ahhh, desserts?" Waiting for Stanley to answer, Pam looked at him as her eyebrows curved upward. Dale was unsure what to say, so he picked his hat up, looked at it, and put it back on the chair.

She stared at Stanley, and with puzzlement still in her voice, she said, "Seven-layer chocolate cake, homemade strawberry ice cream, and bread pudding?"

Stanley said, "I'll have the cake and the bread pudding."

Dale said, "I'll have today's special, tea, and cake with a serving of the homemade strawberry ice cream. And I do not need a take-out plate.

Pam walked away without a word. There was an awkward moment of silence between Dale and Stanley. It broke when Stanley's cell phone rang.

He answered, saying, Wh-wh-what? …I'm t-t-trying. Stanley stood up with his phone pressed to his ear and spoke to Dale, "excuse m-m-me." He turned and walked out of the Diner and stood in front of the ambulance.

Dale watched Stanley as his arms and body became animated. He couldn't tell whether he was excited with anger or something else.

He thought how Stanley had spoken and how he had not stuttered while talking to Pam. He decided his earlier judgment of Stanley was wrong.

Even though they had talked about the mission, something was not right. A few days before, Dale had gone online to learn more about stuttering. He wondered how Stanley could shut it on and off.

He turned away from the window as Pam came with the iced tea. As she sat it on the table, she said, "Don't trust Stanley. I have heard he and Dwight are Brutus's men."

When she heard the door open, she became pale and quickly added in a whisper, "Please don't tell Stanley what I said." She quickly walked away.

Stanley sat down, took a swallow of his tea, and said to Dale, "W-w-work can be aggravating s-s-sometimes. P-p-people are never s-s-satisfied."

Pam came with the food and asked, "Do y'all need anything else."

Dale smiled at her and said, "I'm fine."

Stanley, also smiling, said, "Th-th-thanks P-p-Pam."

Pam raised her eyebrows and said, "I'll bring your desserts in a bit." She walked away.

Dale asked Stanley, "How many days do you work before you have a day off?

"It is supposed to be three twenty-four-hour days one week and four twenty-four-hour days the next week. It alternates but sometimes when I am off, I have to be on call," answered Stanley.

In Dale's mind, he was still wondering why the stuttering came and went, but instead of asking the question, he said, "What do you do on your days off."

Sometimes I go fishing locally or drive to Morehead City and fish from the pier. Sometimes I go to Raleigh and rent myself a nice hotel room and do things around town.

It feels good to get away from Stonehope, and Blackstone County said Stanley without one stutter. Then he asked, "What kind of fishing did you do in Canada?"

"Papa and I mostly fished from our small boat. Sometimes we would be lucky enough to catch a walleye, Muskie, or bass. We only caught what we ate," said Dale.

Stanley hoped for more information but continued, "Here, I catch crappie, catfish, and bass. I enjoy bass fishing best. I found a great spot for catching bass near Webb's Mill, but I keep it a secret."

Dale had been watching Pam in his peripheral vision. It appeared as often as she could, she would find a reason to be close to their table. Dale wanted to talk to Stanley about Dwight Gacy, but he didn't want to upset Pam. Dale wanted to be sure Stanley was on the right side of the drug war. The table became quiet as he and Stanley finished their food.

Right on cue, Pam brought their desserts. While Dale was eating his chocolate cake and ice cream, he asked Stanley about E. H. Denton and his family.

Again, without stuttering, Stanley told him about the family. He said, "In the 1700s, the governor of this area gave two-thousand acres to William Lawrence Denton."

Stanley also explained how the family had passed down the land to various male offspring. He told Dale, "E. H. Denton was the only living son when his father died, so E. H.'s father willed the remaining area of the farm to him. The Denton's of other generations had died or sold their property and moved away."

Dale asked, "Why were the properties only willed to men offspring?"

"It seems women could not own property until the 1900s, and even then, the old practices went on without question in some cases. E. H. had four sisters. One lived with him but later died of cancer. Two sisters married and moved away. The younger sister married Martin Webb and lives on the hill beside the Webb's Mill. I guess Larry will get the farm after E. H. dies. He is an only child," said Stanley as he ate the last of his cake.

When Dale finished his dessert, he began to pull his wallet from his back pocket. "I think I'll ride out to see E. H. and his family. I have not been back since they found me, and I would like to thank them again."

Dale laid twenty-five dollars on the table and motioned for Pam to come over. When she arrived, he said, "Keep the change, Pam, and thanks for the great service."

With her southern twang, Pam smiled and said, "Thank you, Cowboy." She added, "Good to see you again, Stanley."

"S-s-sure, P-p-Pam. You are always the b-b-best," replied Stanley.

The two men walked out the door and talked a few minutes when a fuzzy, black puppy walked up and sat beside Dale's boots. Stanley stopped talking and looked down as Dale squatted to pick up the puppy. "What do we have here?" asked Dale.

"Where did it come from?" Stanley questioned.

They both looked around and saw no one. When Pam saw the puppy in Dale's arms, she went outside. Dale asked her, "Do you know who this puppy belongs to?"

"Never saw it before. Aww, it is so cute," Pam cooed.

They all looked around the restaurant parking lot for clues. They saw nothing. Pam walked back inside and asked if anyone had brought a puppy with them. When the patrons indicated they had not, she went to the door and told Dale no one claimed the puppy.

Dale was smiling as he said, "Looks like I have a dog."

"You can have him," Stanley said. "I don't have time for a dog with my hours."

Dale asked, "Do you want to name him?"

Answering quickly, Stanley said, "No. He's your dog."

"Ok, pup, you are officially named Sir Mozart."

Stanley said, "Wh-wh-what?" He was thinking, this guy named his dog using one of my code words. I guess he is the real thing.

"What's wrong, Stanley? You look fuzzled."

Another hearing another code word, Stanley pondered and said, "Dale, we need to talk soon. We have a lot of work to do."

They smiled at each other, shook hands, and got into their automobiles.

Pam watched as Stanley got into the ambulance and Cowboy got into his Dodge truck. She knew Stanley had an Escalade and wondered how Stanley could afford his vehicle and how Cowboy, who came to town with nothing, could afford his truck.

She had a strong urge to warn Cowboy again, but she had to be very careful, or she would be the one to disappear. She had already lost her son to local drug dealers.

Tears filled her eyes as they always did when she thought about Teddy. The only reason she stayed in Stonehope was to avenge her son's death somehow. She would;   yes,   she   would.

EPISODE 9

Dale turned onto the driveway of the Denton's. He saw a pick-up truck, so he assumed someone would be home. A scruffy dog ran towards his vehicle and began barking. Dale put his window down and spoke gently to the dog.

In a few seconds, the dog stopped barking and started wagging his tail. Dale slowly got out and patted the dog, and spoke to him again. The dog followed him as he walked up the front porch steps to the front door.

He knocked on the door, but no one came. He knocked louder and stood there a minute. Dale walked around to the back porch when no one answered the front door as the happy, scruffy dog followed. He knocked on the door.

He did not hear any sounds coming from the house. Dale went to his truck as the scruffy dog tagged along behind him. He bent to pet and said, "Sorry, fellow, I have to leave." The dog looked forlorn.

Disappointed no one was home, he climbed back into his pick-up. He sat in his truck a few seconds before backing out of the driveway. Instead of heading back to Stonehope, he decided to explore Webb's Mill.

As he pulled off the paved road onto the gravel road which led to Webbs Mill, he thought about what his boss, Rodney, told him about the area. *Webb's Mill is no longer a working mill, but it is a local landmark.*

When Dale rounded the curve, he saw a two-story building. The mill sat beside the river, and it was apparent the old boards were still secure, and the building looked sturdy and in good shape.

He drove to the back of the mill and parked in the shade of a giant oak tree. He got out and walked a few feet so he could see the thirty-foot-high dam as the river water ran over it. He stood a moment listening to the water rushing over the dam and crashing onto the rocks below as he thought; the sound of the water is relaxing.

He opened the truck door and lowered the windows enough for the puppy to have plenty of air. Sir Mozart, still curled up on the passenger seat, was asleep.

The sound of the door opening frightened the puppy. Dale spoke softly to him and gently scratched him behind his ears. He assured the pup he would only be gone for a moment.

Dale walked closer to the dam. He heard children laughing and the voices of adults. He stepped closer to the edge, looked down the ten-foot embankment, and saw the white water rushing over large rocks and away from the dam.

As he looked down the slope, he saw E. H., Larry and his children, and two more adults. He looked for a way to get down to where they were. He walked downstream a few feet and saw a rocky path descending to the river below. He carefully placed his feet as he walked down the path of sand and stones and towards the group of people.

The first one to turn around was an older woman he did not recognize. She looked startled, and the blood drained from her face. Her mouth was open as she gripped the arm of the person next to her. He turned to look at Dale and had the same reaction as the woman.

Talking loudly over the crashing sounds of the water, Dale said, "I didn't mean to startle you. I'm Dale Weaver, and I came to see E. H Denton."

When E. H. heard his name, he turned around. He looked at Dale and then at the two standing beside him. The two adults still had not moved or said a word. He looked back at Dale and realized why they were staring.

He had seen it the day they found Dale but again taken aback as he whispered, "My god."

Not knowing what else to do, Dale walked towards E. H. with his hand extended for a handshake. "Hello, Mr. Denton. I am Dale Weaver, the person you helped out beside the road earlier this month."

E. H. took his hand, firmly shook it, and said, "Yes, I remember you. How have you been doing?"

"Fine, Sir," Dale said, relieved E. H. recognized him.

The two older adults were now looking at E. H. He said to them, "This is the fellow we found injured beside the road. I told you about him.

Before E. H. could say anything else, his brother-in-law said, "You didn't tell us he is the spittin' image of Stephen. It's like seeing a ghost."

Dale looked from the man to E. H., waiting to see why the brother-in-law appeared drained of color.

E. H. lied, "Martin, I didn't see the resemblance the first time I saw him, but you are right. It is like seeing a ghost. Martin, this is Dale Weaver." Continuing, he said, "Dale, this is my brother-in-law, Martin Webb, and this is my sister, Dorothy."

By then, Larry and the children had moved nearer to them. Excitedly Skylar said, "The cowboy prince. I knew he would come back."

Dale took his hat off and bowed to Skylar, and then reached to shake Jordan's hand. Then he looked at Larry and said, "Hi man, it's good to see you again."

Larry smiled and shook Dale's hand, saying, "It seems everyone thinks you are a ghost. Please excuse them, but you look almost identical to my cousin, Stephen. He died in Afghanistan nearly a year ago. It is very eerie."

Dale did not know what to say. He just looked from one adult to the other. Jordan spoke and said, "Why do you look like Cousin Stephen?"

Ill at ease, Dale answered him, "I don't know." He turned back to E. H. and said, "I'm sorry."

E. H. said, "You don't have to be sorry, Dale. I've heard everyone has a twin. I guess you found yours. I wish he were here to meet you."

Dale looked at Mr. and Mrs. Webb as they were whispering back and forth. He was trying to think of something to say when Martin spoke, "We don't mean to make you feel anxious, Dale. It is just quite a shock to see someone looking so much like the son we lost." Martin offered his hand.

Dale shook his hand, and Dorothy extended her hand. When he gently gasped her right hand, she placed her left hand on their clasped hands and said, "It's nice to meet you, son." Tears were running down her cheeks.

Dale was not expecting his reactions as tears welled in his eyes. Dale cleared his throat and said, "It's nice to meet you, Mrs. Webb. I don't mean to cause you pain."

Dorothy Webb smiled and said, "Yes, it is a bit painful, but it is a comfort in some strange way. I hope you will visit us sometime, and we'll show you some of Stephen's pictures."

"I would like to, Mrs. Webb. I would like it very much." Dale said.

Jordan asked, "Hey, are we going to fish some more or what?"

Like a choreographed play, all the adults joined the children and began to fish. Larry offered Dale his fishing pole. Dale declined and asked, "Do you think I can bring my puppy down here?"

"Sure," Larry said.

Dale went back up the embankment to the truck and gently picked up his new puppy. Sir Mozart was small enough to tuck in the crook of his arm. He went back down, found a large rock, and sat down. He watched the family and became melancholy.

He had missed this type of childhood and would have never known he missed it if he hadn't come to Blackstone County for his new mission.

When Skylar looked back and saw the puppy, she put down her fishing pole, walked over to Dale, and sat beside him. Soon she was sitting on the big rock holding and talking to Mr. Mozart.

As the afternoon went on, Larry gave Dale an entire history lesson on Webb's Mill. Each felt like they had made a new friend.

Later, while he was driving back to his apartment, he thought, *this day has made me miss Rex more than ever. Rex was the only person like the family he had ever had.*

EPISODE 10

Dale was looking at a manual he had ordered online. It was for a 1957 Bel Air. He had read it from page to page multiple times after he got off work.

Rodney Medlin, the garage owner, told him about the car and offered to drive him to the location. The Bel Air was behind an old tobacco barn in the rural community of Tarboro.

It looked like a pile of rust, but when Dale and Rodney carefully went over the old car, they agreed a lot of sanding and hard work would help bring it back to life.

The problem was none of the neighbors knew who owned the two-acre plot where the car was sitting, and neither man could make out the VIN.

He and Rodney had spent several hours checking county records to see who owned the property. All the surrounding property had owners who were still living, but the plot for which they looked only showed it being willed to a John Brown seventy years ago.

The next day Dale was at Edwards Diner when Larry Denton walked in. He sat beside Dale at the bar. During their conversation, Dale mentioned the car and the problems he was having.

Larry said he had the next day off, and he offered to take Dale to the Raleigh Department of Motor Vehicle.

Dale had found an old 1962 tag in the trunk of the old Chevrolet. It took the young men most of the day to find out the car's last owner, Theodore Morgan.

When Dale returned to the garage the same day, it was late afternoon. However, Rodney wanted to talk to the surrounding neighbors again.

He and Dale drove to Tarboro and went around asking everyone they saw if they remembered Theodore Morgan. They found out he was in a local retirement home. Rodney and Dale left the community and went straight to the Tarboro Retirement Home.

Luck was with them. Theodore Morgan had a sound mind and remembered the old car. To Dale's and Rodney's surprise, the elderly man pulled the title out of an old Bible that sat beside his bed.

Dale and Rodney listened to story after story the older adult told. They weren't' being kind and patient but were genuinely interested in the stories.

When Mr. Morgan finally stopped talking, he agreed to let Dale have the car. Dale tried to explain he was willing to pay the elderly gentleman any price he asked.

But Theodore Morgan told Dale he wanted to see the old Bel Air painted and hear the engine purr. He also asked to ride in the car one more time. They shook hands in agreement, and the next day Dale picked up the Theodore Morgan and carried him to have the title changed.

Dale looked at the old Coca Cola clock above the garage work bench; it was 11:45. Rodney had said he would be there at twelve. Dale closed the book and turned when he heard the garage door open. It wasn't Rodney.

"Hey, man! Are you working today?" asked Stanley.

"Stanley, good to see you," replied Dale.

Both men walked toward each other and gave a firm handshake. In a couple of weeks, Dale had been in Stonehope; he felt a close friendship with Stanley.

Often Dale visited Stanley and discovered he was a great cook in the kitchen and on the outdoor grill. During these times, they sometimes talked in generalities about the mission. However, Dale's mission contact has not verified Stanley's authenticity.

Considering Stanley's reaction when he named his pup Mr. Mozart and used the word fuzzle Dale was relatively sure Stanley was the right person. However, he felt Stanley was holding back. Rex lost his life because he and Dale trusted the wrong person. Dale wanted to be unquestionably sure about Stanley.

After the handshake, Dale told Stanley what he and Rodney were going to do. He invited Stanley to go with them to pick up the car. While they were talking, the garage door opened, and Rodney said, "Come on. I've got this tow truck for four hours."

All three men climbed into the tow truck and headed to pick up the old Bel Air. They were excited as if they were three little boys on Christmas morning. They left the garage yard talking and laughing.

When Dale, Rodney, and Stanley returned, Dale texted Larry to tell him they had picked up the old Bel Air. Larry returned the text immediately, saying he wanted a ride when the old car was refurbished. Larry also said to let him know if there were anything more he could do.

Dale read the text and smile. Dale sent Larry an emoji of a fisherman with an enormous fish.

EPISODE 11

On the morning of Nine-Eleven, Stanley awoke, set up in the bed, and panicked. Being summoned to the old house on the river was always a bit terrifying. He hated to go, but he had no choice.

When Mad Dog said to meet him, you had to go or else. The or else was what bothered him. In Stonehope, by the time you were in high school, every student had heard about the old house on the river. There were a lot of stories around, and most of them were all true or partially accurate.

Stanley looked at the clock. He had three hours before the meeting. His visit with Mad Dog was more of an inquisition. Stanley knew Mad Dog would ask about Dale, but Stanley would play dumb.

From what Mad Dog said, he had only found the basics on the internet. Stanley would keep other things that he had learned to himself. All things were not for Mad Dog's ears.

Even though they had spoken about their mission, Stanly had to be perfectly sure Dale was authentic. Dale had also used two of his passwords, but Stanley had not verified Dale being his contact: and a mistake could mean his immediate death.

He had called the number to get in touch with his contact, Inrun52, but had not heard from her.

Stanley liked Dale, although he acted oddly at times. One time, they left Dale's apartment on a hot night and walked outside of the garage to find some cool air.

He had asked Dale if he had ever seen the space station going by. Dale had been the one to stutter and asked him if there was a schedule.

He also asked Dale about his parents again, and Dale said, "Yes, one man and one woman," and immediately asked Stanley, "Which comes first? The chicken or the egg?" He wondered if Dale was a private person, but Stanley was sure of Dale having a strange sense of humor.

As Stanley was eating his cereal, he began to think about how he was placed in this situation with Mad Dog. He knew the real identity of Mad Dog and thought it was ridiculous to have to use the made-up name rather than his real name.

When he had to meet him at the river house, Stanley kept from laughing at the man who changed his voice and wore a white hooded cloak like the Ku Klux Klan. However, he knew Mad Dog worked for a cruel madman, so Stanley continued to play the game.

He also knew Mad Dog had access to people who were powerful enough to make anyone disappear. Most locals believed the stories about Mad Dog and his boss were fiction, fabricated to scare people into some weird kind of respect. The scariest part was most of the stories people repeated were woefully accurate.

Stanley remembered the day of his recruitment into the mission. He was in the last days at the community college before becoming a certified paramedic.

He was leaving his last class of the day when his instructor asked him to wait. When all the students left, he said, Mrs. Marshall at the front desk needs to see you.

Clueless his life was about to change, Stanley left the classroom and went to see Mrs. Marshall. When he walked up, she said, "Follow me." He followed her down the hall.

She stopped in front of the janitor's closet. She looked up and down the hall. There was no one. She took a key out of her pocket and unlocked the door.

Stanley remembered rolling his eyes and saying, "If this is one of the students' tricks, I don't have time for it. Tell them to pick on someone else." Mrs. Marshall pushed the door partially open and said firmly, "This is not a prank. Go in."

Stanley remembers going through the door expecting some of his classmates to burst out laughing. He turned towards Mrs. Marshall and gently pushed her aside to go out and face his tormenters.

Before he was out, he heard a noise. He turned to look at the back-closet wall as a section of it opened. It was a hidden door. The person who opened the door walked back to their desk and told Stanley to come in and to sit down; he did.

Instead of facing a bunch of laughing boys, he met the most significant decision of his life. At times he couldn't decide if it was a blessing or a curse.

He couldn't begin to put into perspective the sight of Ms. Tetterton standing behind a small desk. She pointed to the small recorder on her desk and said, "This meeting is recording, Stanley. Please state your name."

Still thinking it was an elaborate trick, he said, "Who's idea was this? Is this an initiation?" Again Ms. Tetterton gruffly said, "State your name." Stanley decided to play along so he could go home; he was hungry. "My name is S-s-Stanley C. Hall."

"What does the C stand for?" Stanley remembered his rush of fear to think the other guys might find out his middle name was Clemus. He sat waiting for the joke to be over.

Ms. Tetterton looked at Stanley with a blank expression and looked at a file lying on the desk, "Stanley, your middle name is Clemus." She looked up and continued, "I have before me your school records as far back as kindergarten. You have always been a good student.

You were, at times, mercilessly teased for your stuttering. Never once did you ever cry or shed a tear in public. You have made all A's in elementary school and high school. You have better than a 4.0 average in your quest to be a paramedic."

"As far as I know, you have never once admitted your grades to any of your fellow students. The only student you associated with in school and out of school was Sunny Tupelo.

The two of you now communicate once in a while. Sunny met you in Raleigh, North Carolina, in a hotel restaurant in May of this year. She was in disguise, and you wore khaki pants, a blue shirt, and a silk tie which Miss Tupelo sent you from France."

Stanley had no idea Ms. Tetterton had been keeping up with him. He knew she had been teaching for a long time. Later he would learn she had been in the area since Sheriff Maddox's marijuana era and before there was an I-95.

Ms. Tetterton's mission; to pave the way for others and to integrate a few home-grown assets to aid the central mission; the expunging of the drug cartels in Blackstone County

Stanley remembered sitting with his mouth open and unable to speak as Ms. Tetterton continued, "Stanley, do you know what your IQ is?" Stanley had shaken his head to indicate no. "It is very high, young man. Your IQ is 190; testing in the third grade and the seventh.

Do you know how I know all these things?" Again, he had shaken his head to indicate no. "My superiors and I have been watching you."

"W-w-why?" Stanley had managed to say.

After the meeting in the janitor closet, Stanley remembered being shocked when Ms. Tetterton told him who she was and why her superiors chose him. She had said, "Do you remember the last time I saw you at your home?"

Before he could answer, she said, "I brought you carrot cake muffins, and we sat at the kitchen table drinking tea. I told you I had recommended you for a particular job. I also said contact would happen at a later time. Stanley, the time is now".

Ms. Tetterton told Stanley she was Inrun52, a special agent sent to help stop drug trafficking along the I-95 Corridor and investigate the killings or disappearances of several people over the last fourteen years, some being agents.

She handed Stanley a list of the things she had planned for him and the name of the person he was to assimilate into the Stonehope community; Dale Weaver.

She told him he would have a job with the rescue squad as soon as he graduated and to be himself. He was to continue hiding his aptitude and his intelligence.

Inrun52 gave him five minutes to decide if he wanted to be an agent. Stanley thought, *why not?* He had been hiding things from others for as long as he could remember, so he didn't see any problem continuing.

After Stanley graduated from community college, he went into training at a guarded place with no name. All he knew was he traveled on a private plane to an area that was primarily mountainous near a rock-filled desert. He was with five other people with names given during training. Stanley's name was Rabbit.

During the nine months of intensive training, he was taught physical and mental toughness, to the point he did not recognize himself. He learned how not to stutter, although advised to keep stuttering as a trait. He learned five different languages and could speak them fluently, some with different dialects.

Stanley became proficient with guns, knives, and other things he could use as a weapon. He learned how to fight combining several martial arts and exposed to endurance tests he felt he would never end

By the last two weeks, only three of the five remained. Stanley had gained muscle mass and could bench press the same as a man twice his size.

The hardest part of his training was watching what happened to captured assets. He learned about all kinds of illegal drugs. He saw the routes some drug dealers customarily used. He watched videos of take-downs and confiscated drugs in everything from a milk truck to a family camper with three small kids.

Some videos were brutal to watch; an unmarked State Patrol vehicle stopped an eighteen-wheeler loaded with pigs headed to New Jersey. The officer and four agents exited the patrol car.

They inspected the truck and confiscated the load of pigs. Immediately the pigs went for an ultrasound. All the pigs stuffed with packages of heroin.

There were videos of drug bust of heroin, cocaine, or marijuana. Some were vehicles carrying untaxed cigarettes and gallons of moonshine or new designer drugs. Even some were undocumented people or young girls and boys slated for the sex trade.

After the training Stanley became an agent and a mole, a silent mole. He was only to talk about what he did and saw if his handler contacted him. He was allowed to pick three safe words he must hear before he should agree to debrief.

Stanley chose fuzzle, jirble, and Mozart. His mission could be tomorrow or ten years away. He had no way of knowing. He kept gathering information mentally.

He never wrote anything down. He had seen things and heard things he kept secret for two reasons. First, he could be debriefed at any time, and second, Mad Dog, Brutus, and Brutus' hogs. Hogs were feed meat, sometimes starved to eat humans, deemed to disappear, bones and all.

Fifteen minutes before the meeting, Stanley said a prayer and headed to the old house on the river to be blindfolded before he went into the house. Playing ignorant and slow was a blessing because he recognized the man on his first visit with Mad Dog.

Stanley thought it was comical for a man he already knew to have a name like Mad Dog. He had to control his smile when the Mad Dog talked.

EPISODE 12

E. H. Denton and his brother-in-law, Martin Webb, sat in the back yard under a Dogwood Tree with their large glasses of sweet iced tea. Being together on this date had turned into a tradition.

They had been sitting in the same place on the first Nine–Eleven. Suddenly Larry rushed out of the house and called for them to come in. He was in a panic, and both of the older men surmised something terrible had happened inside the house.

When E. H. and Martin rushed into the back door, Larry pointed to the television and yelled, "Look at this. Look what is happening."

Larry's dad and his Uncle looked at the television unbelievingly. They walked closer just as the plane crashed into the second of the twin towers.

"God no," said E. H. He said it not as an expletive but as a plea. He was a religious man, a good man, and could not believe what he saw.

He didn't say anything else. E. H. sat down in his recliner, leaning forward, watching and listening just as hundreds of thousands of other people across the United States watched.

Martin sat on the sofa beside Larry with his hands on his knees. His fists gripped so tightly his knuckles looked as if they would protrude through his skin. He was silent.

They sat there a long time and only looked away when they heard the back door open. It was Katherine and her mother-in-law, Sadie. They had taken Jordan for a check-up.

The three men turned to see the women. Sadie said, "We saw part of it on the television at the doctor's office. It's just terrible."

Larry got up and went to his crying wife. He kissed her on the cheek and asked, "Is he OK?" Katherine sniffed and said, "Yes, he is great. He's gained one pound, eight ounces."

Larry used the corner of the baby's blanket and wiped the tears from his wife's face. She smiled, kissed his cheek, and put Jordan in his father's arms.

Katherine walked over to E. H. and kissed his cheek and then did the same to Martin. To them, it was a confirmation they all were in pain for their Country.

They watched the television until the baby began to fuss. It was time for his feeding. As Katherine warmed the milk, the adults began to talk to each other in low tones.

It was as if they were at a funeral. The mood was somber, but everyday life continued even though each realized what they watched in real-time would change their Country forever.

Two weeks after the towers went down, Martin's son, Stephen, came home one afternoon and told his mother and father he had signed to join the United States

Marines. He was leaving the community college and his classes in computer science to fight for his country.

Dorothy Webb fell to her knees and began praying for God to look after her son. She had lived with the fear of war while her husband, Martin, was in Viet Nam. She knew the pain and stress of being in fear every day and knowing the person you loved may not come home.

Martin was proud of his son, but he knew what war could do to a man even if he survived. He looked at his wife and knew they both would be doing a lot of praying until their son came home to them.

Stephen's enlistment was one of the reasons Martin joined E. H. on September eleventh every year. Their son had come home, home and buried in the family cemetery with military honors.

EPISODE 13

Vernon Maddox pulled his patrol car into the driveway, got out, and got into his old 1985 Ford pick-up truck. He drove to the ABC store, purchased two-fifths of Jack Daniels, and headed for the Hardee's drive-thru. It was four o'clock and unusually early for him to leave work, but he had a heavy burden on his mind.

It was her birthday, and it threw him for a loop. After he paid for the food, he drove back onto the street and headed home, anxious to find an envelope in his mailbox.

Today his radio turned to a station that played timeworn Country music. Each song was as if he was punishing himself by listening to the music, which brought back memories.

It was ironic that country music returned her memories because every time she was there, she was listening to a radio station that played blues.

When Junior left for college Vernon's sister, Agnes, moved out of the house. She told him she would find a person to come in to do the housekeeping and laundry. He had refused.

A few months later, Junior came home to find the house nasty and in disarray. He called his Aunt Agnes to find someone to clean Vernon's house. Junior told her he would pay for the cleaning and wanted someone coming every week. Vernon was not happy to be forced to let someone into his home.

Pearl was there cleaning; Vernon walked in and immediately became angry with his sister, Agnes. How could she bring that nigger woman into his house? Vernon had turned and walked out of the house, slamming the door behind him.

He returned a few hours later and found the house cleaner than it had ever been, and it smelled like lavender. All his clothes had been picked up and washed, and there were four covered bowls on the kitchen table. He removed the foil coverings and found fried chicken, potato salad, navy beans, and homemade biscuits.

There was also a note on the table saying, "Mr. Vernon, when you finish your meal, please put the leftovers in the refrigerator so you can enjoy them again. You can use the microwave to heat what you want. Miss Agnes told me what you liked. I hope you enjoy it. I will be back this Friday.

Miss Agnes also told me to leave a bill for the amount I charged for cleaning, the groceries, and the microwave I purchased. I will take cash or a check. You can put it on the table Friday morning. Pearl James."

Soon Vernon enjoyed his clean clothes, clean house, clean sheets, and bed covers. Mostly, he enjoyed the food: Chicken pastry, Venison Stew, Country ham and biscuits, barbecue beef ribs, pork roast, fried or barbecue chicken, and cornbread; all the foods he loved.

Later Pearl started leaving a pie, or cake, or sweet potato jacks. Vernon overlooked her race and enjoyed the work she did and the meals she made for him. However, he still would not be in the house when she was there.

Everyone knew Vernon Maddox was a racist. If you were not white, he would find a way to belittle the person or would insinuate you were not as good as white people. What they did not know was Pearl slowly continued winning Vernon's respect and gratitude.

Vernon began coming home early on Tuesdays and Fridays. If the meal were already on the table, he would eat, and if not, he would take a shower, put on clean clothes and watch whatever was on television until Pearl called him for the meal.

For months he did not speak to Pearl James. If she tried to start a conversation, he would just look at her without saying a word. Later he began talking to her but only when she would ask him what he would like for her to cook.

After a few more months, he thanked her for the meals. One day he shocked himself when he asked her where she lived. Pearl just answered his question and did not try to initiate another conversation.

This went on for almost a year. Vernon became comfortable with the arrangement. He would sometimes leave her a note on the kitchen table about something he wanted her to clean or something he would like her to cook.

Pearl's appearance had not escaped Vernon. He tried to ignore how she held herself with pride and dignity and how she dressed in a neat pair of slacks and a collared shirt.

He became angry at himself when he watched her walk, or bend to pick up something, or how she stood on her toes to reach something in the top cabinet.

Vernon started reminding himself she was a nigger. Then he would reason with himself about why he was attracted to her. After all, she was a very light-skinned nigger. She never made a move or said anything which made him like her, but he did like her.

One day when he came home, she was laughing when he walked in. The sound was melodic, and he caught himself before he said something he would regret.

She turned when she heard the screen door slam. Without missing a beat, she said, "Sorry, Mr. Vernon, they just said something funny on the radio, and I couldn't help but laugh."

Before he could respond, she began telling him what was said. Vernon was not able to control himself, and he started laughing. From that moment forward, Vernon never saw Pearl as a black woman again. He saw her as Pearl, a hardworking, respectable, sometimes funny, and a good-looking woman.

As months passed, they began to have conversations about all kinds of things. Vernon realized Pearl was a knowledgeable woman, and it amazed him. Sometimes

Pearl would stay past her work hours and eat supper with him as they talked and laughed.

Vernon began to gain weight and went less and less to the ABC store. The deputies and other people started to comment on how good he looked. Some had the nerve to tell him he acted 'happy.' However, no one would even think it was because of his black housekeeper; no one…not his sister or son.

One day Vernon walked into the house, and there was no music. The oven was on, and there were two pots on the stove with lids rattling because of the steam. He turned the burners off and opened the oven door.

He could see a roasted chicken. It looked done, so he turned off the oven and then noticed the dishes and utensils stacked on the table. He was puzzled. Pearl had never done this before.

 He stood there in the quiet. Then he heard it; the soft crying. He followed the noise to the living room. Pearl was sitting on the couch with a box of tissues on her lap.

Vernon felt something he rarely felt; sympathy. He walked closer to Pearl and laid his hand on her shoulder. She looked up at him. He was speechless for what felt like a long time as they just looked at each other.

Pearl broke the silence, "Mr. Vernon, I'm sorry. I'll go finish your supper now."

As she tried to rise, Vernon kept a firm hand on her shoulder. He sat down beside her and put his arm around her. At first, she was tense, but she gave in to

Vernon's show of concern in a few seconds and leaned against him. Neither knew how long they sat there. Pearl was the first to move. She sat up and moved a small distance away from Vernon.

She turned and looked at Vernon, and he looked at her beautiful brown face one second, and the next second they were in a passionate kiss and embrace. Something primal held them together as they made their way to Vernon's bedroom.

One-fifth of Jack Daniels was half empty, and the bag of food still sat on the table. Vernon's mind was blurring the past into dark thoughts. He was empty. He had been painfully alone since she left. His life had been whole for several more months after the day they kissed and made love.

Pearl still came only on Tuesdays and Fridays, but he had started coming home during those days to have their time together. They made love, laughed, and talked. She even tried to encourage him when he was down, but it seemed they could never have enough time together. She never asked for more, but he knew she wanted more.

Vernon even thought of taking all the money he had accumulated over the years and taking her somewhere to live everyday life.

He was scared, scared he would never be enough, frightened she would get tired of him, and terrified she would be ashamed of him.

Vernon threw back another glass of whiskey. It was her birthday, and he had only seen pictures of the little girl they created. Pearl has kept her pregnancy a secret until he noticed she had gained weight.

At first, he supposed it was the same reason he gained weight; they were happy. Then one day, he was looking at her from the side. He asked her, "Pearl, are you pregnant?"

Pearl had burst out crying and said, "I'm sorry, Vernon. I'm so sorry. I was trying to be careful."

Vernon still remembered how he felt, and he remembered every word of their conversation. The only times he couldn't remember were the times when he passed out. However, during all the waking hours, he carried the pain of being without Pear and never seeing their daughter.

The day he found out Pearl was pregnant, Vernon had gone to her and put his hand on the child growing for six months. He had used his other hand to wipe her tears. The love he felt for Pearl and their baby was so great he felt as if he would explode.

He took her to the bedroom, and after they made love, he told her they would move away. He asked her for two weeks to get things set up. She had just stood there shaking her head and saying no.

The rest was a blur. Vernon remembered begging Pearl to go away with him. He remembered her putting her hands on each side of his face as she said, "I will think about it." Then she had dressed and left.

The next time Vernon heard from Pearl, it was in an envelope in his mailbox. He opened it. It was a picture of a baby girl. Pearl had written on the back of the picture, "Born October 3, 7 pounds, 3 ounces. Name Vernel Pearl Maddox."

Vernon sat down at the table and cried. Pearl had sent a picture every year since then. Vernon thought he would never see anyone as beautiful as Pearl until he saw their daughter.

There was never a return 0address, only a Baltimore postmark. He respected Pearl enough not to bother her. She never asked for money. He just hoped she had a good life.

After receiving the first photo, he opened an account in a Raleigh bank in Vernel's and Pearl's name. He has left the information in his will. Junior would be handling it. He hoped Junior would find her and give her the money.

Vernon's head drooped until it finally landed on the table. He did not feel it. He did not feel anything for the next four hours.

EPISODE 14

Dale drove into the drive of Edward's Diner, where he planned to have lunch. He had been coming to the Diner for at least one meal a day.

Not only was the food good, but he enjoyed hearing the local patrons talking. Most of the time, people ignored him, but occasionally some would stare and then whisper; he was still an outsider.

He was thinking about the people who whispered as he reached for the door handle, and it wasn't there. He looked up and saw her face again, a beautiful face. The same shock he had the first time he saw her traveled through his body. He stood back so Katherine could come out the door.

Dale just stared for a moment and then said, "Mrs. Denton, it is a pleasure to see you."

Katherine smiled, thinking Dale Weaver acted like a young boy. She said, "I heard you joined the family fishing adventure the other day. Skylar talks about the cowboy prince and Sir Mozart all the time, and you seem to be a hero to my son."

"You have a very nice family," Dale said, feeling foolish. His mind was not working correctly, and he hated what Katherine did to him.

Dale tipped his hat and moved to the side so Katherine could continue out the door. When she passed him, the smell of her raced to his brain with pictures flashing; he knew they would never be.

Just as the aroma of her hit, she stopped and said, "Please come to see us soon so we can catch up with what you are doing. Larry said you had the reputation of being the best mechanic around."

"Thank you. I'll try to get out there soon. And...and...thank you for taking care of me the night I was hurt."

Katherine smiled sweetly and said, "We were glad to help. Now, hurry and come to see us. Larry is excited to see the Bel Air coming in the driveway." She pulled her keys out of her purse and walked to her car without looking back.

When Katherine was in the car, Dale gave a wave, turned, and walked into the restaurant. He looked around and saw a table of four older women looking at him.

He looked around for a table or booth. They all had customers, so he walked to the bar and took a seat. It was within hearing distance of the four women. He removed his hat and placed it on the stool beside him. The women began talking.

One of the women said, "Have Y'all seen the newest movie with Sunny Tupelo?"

Another voice said, "Janie and I went to see it, but it was too bloody, and why did they have to make the soldier Sunny fell in love with a white boy."

A voice that sounded older than the other two said, "Jackie, you know times have changed. We see the same thing all the time, especially when we go to the malls in larger towns.

And, don't forget our sheriff and what he did. Sunny is a great actress. Me? I'm proud to see a hometown girl make it big. She always was a lovely girl."

"She is not a hometown girl. She moved from here before she graduated from high school. She didn't become famous until she moved to Raleigh."

Dale was so intent on listening he did not hear or see Pam walk up to the counter. Pam said, "Hey, Cowboy. Where are you?"

Looking up at Pam, he smiled his biggest smile. "Pam, I was thinking about an auto part order. How are you?"

"I'm great today. I get one weekend a month off, and this is the weekend," Pam said as she returned the smile."

"What do you have planned?" Dale asked.

"Nothing special," She said and then added, "What can I get for you today?"

Dale ordered and continued listening to the women at the table next to him. "You have to admit Sunny has done well in Hollywood. Who would have guessed a girl like her would have made it so big?"

Pam walked over to the women's table with the change from all four tickets. She thanked the ladies and walked back to the kitchen window, and picked up Dale's order.

The women stood and walked away from their table as Pam brought the food to Dale. Dale looked at her and said, "Pam, I want to go to Raleigh tomorrow night and eat somewhere really nice with good food. Maybe we could see the new movie with Sunny Tupelo."

Immediately Dale realized what he said. He looked at Pam and started to apologize. Pam was already laughing.

"Really? You don't like the food here?" Pam teased.

Dale stuttered, "Ahh, yes. I come here almost every day."

Pam turned her head away from Dale as Cooksey called her name. "I'll be back in a minute," She said without looking back at Dale.

Dale ate his giant burger and his onion rings as he watched Pam rush from behind the counter to take care of patrons. When he finished, he motioned for Pam to come over. When she walked over, she asked, "Any dessert today?"

"No. Not today." He answered, and with his biggest smile, he said, "Can I talk you into going to Raleigh with me tonight. I need a copilot. I've not driven in Raleigh. Larry Denton took me to the license bureau a while ago, but I couldn't tell him how to get back out of the city. He thought it was funny." Dale gave her his biggest smile and said, "And, I need help finding good food." They both laughed.

Then Pam's eyes widen, and the pupils became larger. She looked into Dale's haunting blue eyes without saying a word, but her mind was running wild with her romantic scenarios.

After a long pause, she said, "I can give you the address of the best steak house in Raleigh, and you can use your GPS."

Dale said, "I would like to have a human talking to me. Besides, I may want to go to the movie while I'm there. Will you please go?" Dale asked.

He had no idea of his effect on women. He didn't realize his dark skin, slightly curly black hair, his full eyelashes, his sky-blue eyes, and his deep voice had any effect on women.

"Why me?" Pam asked.

"Why not you? Dale said.

Pam took a deep breath and slowly released it between pursed lips and then said, "Sure, Dale. I'd love to go."

"Tell me what time and where to pick you up."

After Pam wrote her address on an unused ticket, she handed it to Dale and said, "You tell me what time."

"How about seven?" He asked.

"Don't be late, Cowboy." She teased.

He laid a twenty on the counter and said, "Keep the change." He looked straight into Pam's eyes and said, "I'm looking forward to the trip. See you tonight."

After Dale walked out the door, Pam took another deep breath and held it for a moment before noticing the person in booth seven waving his hand to get her attention. She rushed over, leaving her trembling legs and the butterflies in her stomach behind.

Dale sat in his truck outside the restaurant, looking at nothing. The interaction with Pam made him think of Rex. Rex believed himself to be a Don Juan, and it was his downfall. He had no control when it came to women.

Dale had been with a few women during his go-fast-boat days, but the only one he cared to remember had come to him one night before a huge shipment trip. He sat in his truck with his mind in another world, thinking about his first night with Madeira.

He was leaving from a remote area on a beach in Columbia. Each trip was usually a several hundred-million-dollar haul of heroin and Columbian Gold.

He and Rex were island hopping until they were in international waters southeast of Key West. They would wait for other boats to come from the islands or the mainland to take their part of the shipment. Any shipment left over would be dumped into the international waters, and Dale and Rex would make their way back to Columbia.

The first of several nights with Madeira was a sweltering and humid night. Since it was before a big run, Dale was anxious and didn't expect to sleep. Rex was off with a hooker.

Dale lay across the bed in the little house where he and Rex lived. He heard someone whispering in broken English with a strong local dialect, "Senior, my name Madeira. I here to ease your mind. I not here to hurt you."

Dale immediately grasped his Glock, which lay beside him. He quickly racked the slide.

"Senior, please don't shoot." He heard a flick and saw a small lighter with a flame. The flicker of the lighter showed a petite beautiful young woman beside the bed.

She was creamy brown with long black wavy hair, and she smelled like jungle flowers. Her eyes were black and sparkling as they mirrored the flame.

Dale asked, "Who sent you?"

"Nadie me ha enviado." She said and then added in her broken English. I see you in the, ahh, mar-ket. You kind and feria. I get you bebé en mi vientre. She patted her belly as she was talking.

Dale had seen her in the market several times with an older woman but again asked, "No one sent you?"

Madeira shook her head fiercely while saying, No, Senior Weaver. Want bebé.

Intrigued, he asked, "Por qué?"

Her smile shown in the flickering flame as her face turned into a frown and her brows puckered. "You no want Madeira?"

"Why do you want to be with my child, Madeira?" Dale asked again.

Hesitantly she said, "Quiet man with bonita face make good bebé.

Dale couldn't help but laugh. He reached out his hand and said, "Lay with me."

She walked closer and touched his hand, picked it up, and pressed it against her lips. He felt paralyzed, body and mind. He allowed her to continue.

Remembering did not make him feel guilty but appreciative. She, the dark dream of the night, was wild but tender. He had fallen asleep with her pulled to his body, cupped like other lovers in history.

When he awakened later, she was gone and Rex was calling him to get up.

He was confused. He heard someone calling to him. He looked to the side and saw Pam as she yelled through the window, "Are you having truck troubles?"

"Ahh, no. I was just thinking about something I had to pick up for Rodney."

Pam shrugged her shoulders, turned, and walked back into the restaurant.

Later that night, Dale opened the door of the Red Lobster. As they walked in, Pam looked at him and said, "There are a lot of people waiting. Do you want to try somewhere else?"

It's OK with me. We can go to the bar and wait. I imagine most places will have waiting times on Saturday night," he said.

They sat down at the bar. "What do you want," Dale asked.

"Sex on the Beach," Said Pam.

Dale sat there looking at Pam as his face drained color. He did not move. Not even a twitch. A picture of Madeira in his arms on a beach ticked through his mind as if it were a scene in the movie, From Here to Eternity. It was so vivid he felt Pam could see it.

Pam just stared back. She didn't know whether to laugh or repeat it. The bartender saved them both when he came over and asked, "What can I get the lady?"

Pam smiled and said, "Sex on the Beach, please."

And you, Sir?

"Amaretto and Coke," said Dale. The bartender walked away, and Dale turned back to Pam. "Sorry, I'm not familiar with girly drinks."

She laughed and said, "Oh my god, I didn't know. Sorry."

He laughed too. The bartender brought over their drinks, and he tasted his thinking how it tasted like Dr. Pepper; Dr. Pepper was his favorite. Before they started a conversation, a table was available.

They ordered, and Pam started the conversation by saying, "You've been here a few months. I assumed you would have left Blackstone County by now."

"You've been keeping up with me?" He said with a big smile.

It is not difficult because Dwight and Stanley brought you to the Diner on August 4th. I remember because it was my birthday and I was upset because I had to work. You made my day when I saw a good-looking cowboy come in."

"August 4th is my birthday too." Said Dale

"No, it is not," declared Pam.

"Yes, it is. My birthday is the same as yours," Dale exclaimed.

"Well, I guess it wasn't so bad working on my birthday. It was better than getting bashed in the head as you did."

The waitress came with their tea, and after she left, Pam asked, "What year were you born?"

"A long time ago."

Pam smiled and said, "Yeah? I think I am older than you."

Dale looked puzzled again as he said, "Why does it matter?"

Shrugging her shoulders, Pam said, "Guess it doesn't." Then she changed the subject. "Looks like you and the Denton family have become friends. When I saw you with Larry, E. H., and the kids the other day at the restaurant, Y'all looked like you were having a good time."

With a softer smile, Dale said, "Yes, I have eaten with them a few times and been with them fishing several times at Webb's Mill. Larry and I went to Dicks Sporting Goods Store here in Raleigh a couple of weeks ago.

I didn't know there was so much outdoor stuff. We were in there for almost three hours. I spent way too much money. I even bought two tents so Larry, the kids, and I could go camping.

Their food came as Dale talked about how much he enjoyed being with the kids and how much he enjoyed being a cowboy prince. Of course, he had to explain the story of how he received the name.

Pam looked at him as he talked about the Denton family and could see he had become good friends with them. In her mind, she thought he could have picked some bad friends like Dwight Gacy and some of his buddies.

She had seen Dale several times in the restaurant with Stanley, but Stanley was hard to read lately. She internally questioned why he stuttered sometimes and sometimes he did not. She decided to ask Dale what he thought about it.

Pam's and Dale's conversation went on after their meal was over. Dale looked at his watch and said, "It will be time for the last movie soon. Do you want to go?"

As if on cue, the waiter came back with the check. Dale gave him cash for the meal and a generous tip. Dale looked at the waiter and said, "Thank you."

"Thank you, Sir. We thank you for dining with us. Have a good night."

When they were in the car, Dale turned to Pam and said, "I have put the theater address in GPS. We should make it there in time?"

Pam replied, "Good, I want to see this too."

Later, they discussed the movie on the drive home, and Pam told Dale what she knew about Sunny Tupelo. She also told him the rumors she had heard about Stanley and Sunny Tupelo having a thing.

When they were a few miles from her house, she said, "I would ask you inside, but I'm getting up early tomorrow to visit my friend, Sea, in Zebulon?"

"Oh, OK." Dale didn't feel disappointed. He felt relieved. He turned to her and gave her one of his biggest smiles and said, "Who is Sea? Isn't it an unusual name?

Pam laughed and said, "That will have to be another conversation another time."

"Good, it means you will go out with me again?"

"Sure," Pam said as she opened her door.

Dale quickly got out and walked a few feet to her front door. When they reached her door, she said, "I had a great time, Dale. I don't know who can talk the most, you or me."

Dale leaned forward and gently kissed Pam on the cheek and then said, "You do!"

They both started laughing. Pam opened her door and went inside. After Dale heard the lock, he turned around and walked back to his car, thinking about how much fun it was to have a female friend with whom he could talk.

EPISODE 15

E. H. watched Larry as he held Katherine's hair dryers. It was a comical sight. Larry didn't see him smile because he tried to make sure all the paint was dry on Jordan's homemade Halloween costume.

"Daddy, is it dry yet? I need to get dressed," said Jordan.

"Just a few more minutes, son. We don't want to have paint on the car seats."

Skylar burst through the door and twirled until she tripped and fell against her daddy. Jordan's costume slid across the room. Jordon screamed, "Skylar, you ruined my Lego block costume."

Larry jumped up to retrieve the costume as Katherine walked in and said, "What in the world is going on in here?"

Skylar was crying as Jordan told his mother, "Skylar ruined my Lego block costume! Now I don't have anything to wear to the church Fall Festival."

E. H. sat at the table, taking it all in. He thought, *this is life, and ain't it sweet*. He knew it was better to stay out of the way. He chuckled.

Katherine heard E. H. chuckle and turned to give him the evil eye. As she did, Larry spoke up, "Jordan, your costume is not ruined, so stop crying. Come here and let me put it on."

Katherine said, "No, wait until we get to the church. We will put it on before he goes in. I don't believe he can wear his seat belt if he puts it on now."

"Aww, Mama, Skylar has hers on; it's not fair."

Larry looked at Katherine and then at Jordan before saying, "Jordan, do you remember how long it took us to make your costume?"

Jordan shook his head and whined, "Yes."

Before anyone else could say anything, E. H. stood up and said, "Do you remember when you made the fort using boxes glued together, and I wanted to lay it in the back seat, but you tried to hold it while I was taking you to school?

"Yes, sir."

"What happened to it, Jordan?"

"You had to stop fast for the deer that ran across the road, and I dropped it. It broke."

E. H. walked over to Jordan and got down on one knee. "Listen, son; sometimes adults can see things which might happen. Your mother sees these things, Jordan, so don't argue with her."

"Yes, Sir."

Katherine glanced at E. H. this time with thankful eyes and said to Larry, "Will you hold Jordan's costume while I drive?"

In a few minutes, E. H. was on his way to the church in his pick-up truck full of pumpkins. As he followed his family in Katherine's car, he reflected that the only thing that *would top this off is if Sarah was with us.*

His eyes teared, and he took his handkerchief from his jacket pocket and wiped his tears away but not the pain.

EPISODE 16

Stanley sat at the table, waiting for his coffee maker to finish brewing its eight cups of coffee. Stanley purchased the maker for himself on his last birthday.

He liked the coffee maker because he could program it to begin brewing at 5:39 AM. Stanley was an early riser, but he was slow to be fully awake.

The morning after a busy Halloween night was tough. Stanley didn't get to bed until 3:00 AM. No matter what time he went to bed, he always woke at 5:30.

When he finished his first mug of black coffee, he made himself sausage, eggs, toast, grits and replenished his cup with coffee. He turned on the small TV he kept in the kitchen, set the table for one, took the peach preserves from the frig, and sat down to his meal.

Once he finished, he began clearing the table. He heard something, and it was not the TV. He muted the sound and listened.

Stanley ran to the bedside table and pulled out a metal, locked box. He dialed in his four-number combinations. His secure phone was ringing; he keyed in the code number and said, "Hello."

"Hello, Rabbit, this is Inrun52."

"Hello, Ms. T-t, I mean Inrun52. I have been waiting for your call.

"Yes, I know. How was your visit with Mad Dog?"

"Mainly, he wanted to know about Dale Weaver. I want to talk to you about Dale. He has thrown out two of my passwords, but I don't know whether to trust him or not."

Inrun52 said, "He named a little pup he found Mozart. Very imaginative, don't you think?"

"Yes, Mam," He said as he wondered how she knew.

"I have an assignment for you. Get paper and pen and write down what I tell you. When you have finished writing it down, you must read it and then tear it into tiny pieces and flush it down the commode." Said Ms. Tetterton knowing Stanley had a photographic memory.

"Yes, Mam," Said Stanley. "Just a moment." Stanley went to a kitchen drawer and pulled out a small pad of paper and a pen. "I'm ready."

His handler talked slower than usual to make sure Stanley had time to write down what she was telling him. When she finished, she said, "Rabbit, read every word to me."

Stanley read what was on the paper and asked, "Did I get it all correct, Mam?"

"Yes. Have you memorized it?"

"Yes, Mam."

"What did I tell you to do with it?"

"You told me to tear it into tiny pieces and flush it down the commode."

"Do it now."

Stanley tore the paper in the tiniest pieces he could, put them in the commode, and then flushed it. When the water stopped running into the tank, he flushed it again. He walked back to the phone and said, "I have done what you asked."

"Excellent, Stanley. I'll see you soon.

EPISODE 17

Dale woke up from a good night's sleep with no dreams he could remember. For a moment, he believed he heard rain. Dale rolled over towards the light coming from the window and realized he was listening to the ocean. He swung his legs to the side of the bed and sat there gathering his thoughts.

It was Sunday, the day after their deep-sea fishing trip. He, Stanley, and Larry had spent the whole day deep sea fishing. They began catching a few Wahoo, Blackfin Tuna, and a few other smaller varieties about an hour out. The run lasted for over three hours, and then the search began again.

After the Wahoo stopped, they began eating the sandwiches and apple pie E. H. had sent. The deckhands began clearing and preparing for another run.

The three fishermen laughed and joked about who had caught the biggest fish. They were happy with their catch. They watched the water behind the boat as the captain made large circles in the cold ocean water.

The November day began in the low forties with full sunshine. The three men were dressed for a colder day but had deposited their jackets in the cabin of the fishing vessel when it became warner. After the meal, the men went to the deck, and each sat in a fighting chair.

One of the crew members began to throw chum into the water behind the boat. Everyone kept an eye on the following sea and beyond. In a few minutes, Stanley jumped up and yelled, "Sailfish."

The crew had set up the reels and rods for possible sharks as they slowly headed back to the dock. Just as Stanley yelled, one of the reels began smoking. The fish was running away from the boat.

The crew member helped Stanley secure the rod to the chair. Dale and Larry were on their feet yelling for Stanley to hang on as the Sailfish jumped out of the water, appearing to fly in slow motion.

Dale stood and walked to the window to see the sun gleaming on the waves. His mind jumped back into his go-fast-boat days and Rex.

He wished Rex had been on the fishing trip the day before. He and Rex had been on several fishing trips, but the shark Rex always wanted to battle and catch had eluded him.

Dale heard noises from the floor below. He squinted, shook his head, and willed the memories to go away. He dressed and went down the stairs to see Larry and Stanley drinking coffee.

"Morning," Dale said as he opened the refrigerator to get the orange juice.

Stanley said, "Do you want to go with us to get breakfast?"

"Sounds good," Dale said as he put the juice back into the frig.

Stanley stood and said, "I'm going to drive, and so is Larry because he will be leaving the restaurant to go home. He needs to be there in time for his shift."

"Do you want to ride with me, Dale?" asked Larry.

Dale rubbed his unshaven face and answered, "Sure. I wish you didn't have to go."

"Yeah, me too," Larry said as he reached for his overnight bag and his truck keys. "We will do another trip in a few weeks. Maybe we can go further south next time."

As the men were walking out the door, they began planning for their next fishing trip.

EPISODE 18

Detective Cain snapped his fingers, and the screen went blank. "Ok, guys. We don't have much to go on, but this piece of trash stayed within a hundred-mile radius for the body dumps."

"Four of the women are identified and lived close to their dumping spot. We believe he knows the area since he always dumps his victims on an unpopulated road."

"However, he also chooses a spot where he does not have to leave the pavement. He may be someone you know, someone who has lived here all his life."

"Or, he may be someone who just came to this area. It is a real possibility since the first body is not identified."

Sheriff Maddox walked to the area in front of the screen. Everyone was waiting for the usual bashing. When Vernon began to speak, they looked at each other in disbelief.

Vernon cleared his throat, and all the men were eyes-forward. In an unfamiliar tone, Vernon said, "The only way we are going to find this monster is if all of you keep your eyes open. Let's get this bastard, dead or alive."

With the voice everyone was used to, Sheriff Maddox said, "Now get the hell out of here and do your damn jobs."

Vernon turned, walked into his office, and slammed the door so hard the glass panels rattled. He locked the door, closed the blinds, and sat in his very uncomfortable chair.

He put his elbows on his desk, propped his head in his hand, and squeezed his eyes shut. He wanted to get the picture of the woman found under the Eagle Creek Bridge out of his mind.

The picture of the shapely, brown-skinned woman reminded him of Pearl. He squeezed his eyes tightly as a tear ran down his left cheek. He let it drop upon the desk. The pain of her being gone was so intense he bit his bottom lip until it bled Even though it's Sunday, Sheriff Vernon Maddox sat at his desk as his ten detectives and twenty-two patrol officers gathered in the open office area. Some sat in chairs, some sat on desks, and some stood; all were waiting for a browbeating.

Vernon was known for his loud, abusive language, but people also knew when something was important to the Sheriff, he would not stop until they solved the case and the perp was arrested or dead. He was like a dog fighting for a bone.

Vernon looked up occasionally and met eyes with some of the men. He had called almost everyone, even the off-duty officers and all his detectives.

It was eight-fifteen and past the time for everyone to be there. Vernon picked up a folder and opened his office door. For a moment, he stood behind his desk. He looked around as the men stopped talking one by one; the ones sitting stood up.

Vernon knew this meeting with everyone in attendance was rare, and he knew he had some of the best detectives and officers in the state. He demanded excellence.

"Look around, men. Is there anyone missing?" The mumbling of the men went around the room as they looked for missing officers.

They were shaking their heads as one office spoke up, "No, Sir. We don't seem to be missing anyone."

Detective Jonas spoke from the back of the crowd, "Sir, Detective Perez is not here. She called me to say she was working on a lead in the Bell murder and wouldn't be here."

The Sheriff rubbed the back of his neck with his left hand, bit his bottom lip, and turned red in the face as he thought, *the token, spic-female, thinks she knows better than I do. I knew she would be trouble.*

No one dared to speak. Vernon held the folder up and said, "In one month, we have had six female murders in surrounding counties, and this morning Blackstone County has its first. It seems to be the same MO as the others."

"The body of a young woman appears to have been dumped on Jones Town Road near the Eagle Creek Bridge. Officer Cain received the call at five this morning."

"An early fisherman walked down the bank and saw the body partially hidden by weeds. He called 911, and Detective Cain and officer Edwards went to the scene."

The Sheriff looked towards Detective Cain and said, "Tell 'em what you found, Jim."

Detective Jim Cain walked to the side of the room where there was a large TV screen. He motioned for the tech to put the first picture on the screen and then said, "Previously notified about the MO of the other murders, this death appears to be by the same son-of-a-bitch."

"I talked to Medical Examiner Smithson after her initial examination. This picture, as you see, shows a lot of cuts. Smithson said there were one hundred and twenty-five cuts from a very sharp knife in varying depths and lengths. Each victim is raped, probably more than once."

"Only one of the cuts would have been fatal, and the ME believes the one between the ribs and straight into the heart was the last one."

"Put up the next picture, Mark. As you can see, this woman's back has a large circular cut with the number eight cut inside the circle."

"The number of cuts and the placements, and the design are almost identical to the six victims."

"The eight-ball design is not and will not be fed to the news media, and we expect you to keep it that way." Everyone was still quiet as another picture showed on the screen. Detective Cain began, "This is a picture from the bridge before the removal of the body. It appears the naked body was dropped from the bridge.

As all of you know, this bridge is on a stretch of road with no houses. The nearest home is over a mile away. Detective Williams and I went over the area very carefully. There were no tracks of a vehicle stopping on the side of the road.

I have talked with the head detective of Marsh County. He said our site sounds like the others. The murderer left no clues; not even DNA, even though each is a rape victim."

.

EPISODE 19

After breakfast with Larry, Stanley drove Dale to see the Oceanana Fishing Pier. It was much colder than it was the day before, and after they exited the Escalade, Stanley and Dale zipped up their jackets and pulled their newly purchased Captain Stacy caps tight to their heads.

Only a few people were fishing from the pier. Stanley and Dale walked down the dock, speaking to each fisherman and an older and very weathered woman.

The weathered woman told the men she had been fishing from the pier every day for twenty years. She then added with a laugh, "I don't fish out here when there is a hurricane in the area." Her stories captivated the two young men, and some made them laugh.

As they talked with her, Stanley looked at his watch. It was near the time for their meeting back at the ocean front house. Inrun52 was probably waiting for them. She was now a handler for Stanley and Dale.

As they rode back to the beach house, Dwight Gacy called Stanley to tell him about the murdered woman he had picked up. He told him the Eight Ball Killer had killed her.

Dwight seemed intrigued with the cuts on the body, which evidently, he had looked at extensively before he transported her to the coroner's office. Stanley shuddered as Dwight told him about the body. He felt Dwight was enjoying telling him the gruesome details.

EPISODE 20

E. H Denton quietly closed the door and stood on the porch with the flashlight in his hand. He inhaled the cool, crisp air of early November.

Soon the sun would be rising. He would wake everyone in time for breakfast and dress for Sunday school and church. His thoughts were also on Sarah. He missed his wife to the point of physical pain.

He turned the flashlight to the steps and walked down to the ground. He heard his Beagle, Ratchet, wiggling through the hole under the porch. Ratchet was quiet, but his tail was swinging back and forth.

He was used to the early morning walks to the famous black boulders called Blackstone for many generations. Mornings like this E. H. used for special prayer time.

Ratchet ran ahead of E. H. just outside of the flashlight beam. He was rushing because he knew what would happen when they returned; a big bowl of dog food.

E. H. began his prayers on the way. As always, he started with thanks, then prayers for his family and then friends. The last prayer was always to be a better Christian.

When E. H. climbed the roughly hewed steps of Blackstone and sat down, he felt closer to God than anywhere he had ever been. Even though he knew the boulder was a special place, he did not understand all the things that happened near it.

The things he did know were puzzles, and he had asked God to explain them. His father told him about the plant-free area located on their farm and what sometimes happened there.

When E. H. looked up, he could see twilight above the treetops. Out loud, he asked, "Did you send me an answer yet, Lord? Help me understand."

EPISODE 21

When Stanley and Dale arrived back at the beach house, the wind had picked up, and the ocean was churning with large crashing waves. It was icy, and both men rushed up the stairs and opened the door to feel the heat.

As the involuntary shivers began to cease, they removed their jackets and hats and hung them on one of the hooks which lined the entrance wall.

As they walked down the short hallway, they smelled the hot chocolate and rounded the corner. Inrun52 was filling three cups.

"Hey Stanley, it is nice to see you again," She said as she gave him a big hug. She looked over Stanley's shoulder; she smiled at Dale as she continued hugging Stanley.

When she let him go, she headed towards Dale and hugged him just as hard, and as long as she did, Stanley said, "I have been waiting years to meet you, son. Your reputation precedes you."

When Miss Tetterton loosened her hug, and Dale stepped back, smiled, and said, "I didn't know handlers could be so nice."

Stanley looked as if he was in shock as he said, "I didn't know you two knew each other."

"Dale and I never met, but I was given all the pertinent information on Dale for years. Besides, even though Dale doesn't know it, he and I are from the same place."

"I didn't know you ever lived in Canada," said Stanley.

Ms. Tetterton smiled at a puzzled Dale and said, "Even though I never met you, Dale, I have known you since you were a small boy. We arrived in Blackstone County the same way but in different times."

Becoming Inrun52, she said, "Let us not talk about it now. Sit down and try this hot chocolate before it gets cold. There are some homemade sugar cookies for us on the table."

The three sit around the table, enjoying the cookies and hot chocolate for a few moments before anyone spoke—each of the young men wondering different thoughts because of what Inrun52 had said.

Dale realized Inrun52 was the same as he was, and she was a part of his mission. Stanley was wondering how Miss. Tetterton had known Dale when he was a little boy, and maybe Dale knew more than he let on.

Dale spoke first, "This hot chocolate is different. It has a kick."

Miss Tetterton laughed as she said, "Yeah, it has a bit of Bailey's Irish Cream in it to keep you warm."

Surprised, Stanley said, "I was beginning to think I was in the twilight zone."

They all laughed, and Inrun52 became serious. I have a lot to go over before I have to leave. Are you ready to get down to business?"

Both said, "Yes, Mam."

Miss Tetterton continued to talk well past lunchtime and three more hot chocolates. However, as hungry as Stanley and Dale were, they listened intently and took mental notes.

She gave them updates on the date of the ultimate takedown of the leading drug ring while leaving out specific details which could get them killed before the takedown took place.

It was not that Inrun52 didn't trust Dale and Stanley, but she knew human instinct might not allow them to go step by step when they knew innocent people might be getting hurt in the meantime.

The total annihilation of the drug traffic along the I-95 would not happen. However, removing the leaders would cause a setback, and it would take the cartel a while to replace all the necessary people for an effective crew.

Mainly, it would give the DEA, the FBI, and the Federation of Planets a chance to install long-term undercover agents who could be a part of the reestablished cartel crew.

After Inrun52 finished talking, she said, "Neither of you should talk about any of this after you leave here. There are so many electronic ways for you to be exposed. We try to protect you the very best we can but the cartel is also searching for new ways to bypass us and track us.

They know there are agents, so the danger of being caught is real. If you are found out or captured, we may not have time to protect you or may not be able to acknowledge you.

"Are there any questions?" Inrun52 asked.

"It is not a question but a concern. You mention Sunny Tupelo would be at one of the events. I am worried about her safety", Stanley said.

"You do not have to worry about her. You and Sunny trained the same way, and she knows about you being an agent.

Her acting abilities help her greatly, and as you know, she has enormous talent. Her training and her travels worldwide are significant assets. Sunny goes to parties and events where some of the important people are also involved in the cartel.

These attributes give her a chance to listen. Like you, Stanley, few realize she is super intelligent and also has total recall. You may keep up your communication as usual, but to protect yourselves, do not change any narrative in your letters or phone conversations," explained Inrun52.

"Dale, do you have any questions?" she asked.

"No, Mam, but I am relieved Stanley, and I are up to date on the same things, and we know we can trust each other. You have explained things well, and I am looking forward to the completion of the mission." Dale answered.

Inrun52 looked at the two men. She placed her right hand on Dale's hand and her left hand on Stanley's hand and said, "God be with you, watch out for Brutus, and keep your eyes peeled. He is very cunning and cruel."

Stanley and Dale looked at each other to say he is much more cunning and dangerous than we contemplated. They were not afraid but were single-minded and determined. Brutus would go down.

Inrun52 stood up and said, "I will contact Stanley if need be. Keep your lives as normal as possible. This process will seem as if it is drawn-out and unhurried, but when things start rolling, it will be like a runaway locomotive.

I know you both are well trained and will be professional as well as effective. Have faith in yourselves."

Inrun52 looked at her watch and said, "My car will be here in one minute. You two stay here tonight and go home in the morning.

This house is clear of all listening and video devices, so you may talk while you are here. Stanley's house is checked for the same devices once a week. If you must speak of the mission, do it at his house."

She grabbed her coat, threw kisses, walked down the hall, down the steps, and into the car. In an instant, she was gone

Stanley and Dale looked at each other, and at the same time, they proclaimed they were famished. They drove to a small restaurant in Swansboro and ate local seafood. They talked about the fisherwoman on the pier and their plans for a different route back home.

Stanley said it would be nice to take the Cherry Branch-Minnesott Beach Ferry at Havelock. He told Dale, "It will take more time, but I enjoy riding the ferry to Minnesott Beach.

It is a small place, and we will be traveling through more small fishing towns. We can also ride to Oriental and look at the boats. I think you will enjoy it. We are going to need some downtime before we get back to our jobs."

"Sounds good to me; I always enjoy new places. What time do you want to leave tomorrow morning?" Dale asked.

"About seven, OK?

Dale agreed, and they made small talk until they arrived at the beach house. There they spent several hours talking about their mission, its dangers, and its purpose. They went to bed at eleven, rose again at six, and took the long way home.

EPISODE 22

It was not light when Sir Mozart woke Dale. While he took Sir Mozart for a walk, his thoughts were about the granite boulder, Blackstone, and E. H. Denton.

As Dale watched his dog searching for the perfect spot to relieve himself, he thought about the first time he met the Denton family on that August morning.

When he reflected on E. H., he saw of a gentle and kind man. He enjoyed spending time with him and his whole family.

Katherine's face appeared in his mind, and he forced himself to think of something else. He knew it was wrong to feel the way he did about Katherine and hated himself for it. She was a married woman and Larry's wife; he respected that.

Dale lost track of time, and it was soon light. He and Sir Mozart had walked several blocks. It was Sunday morning, and the small town of Stonehope was quiet. Dale called to his dog as he turned to retrace his steps back to his apartment.

He soon was thinking about his and Pam's drive to Greenville and their dinner at the Cracker Barrel. The date ended like their others with a kiss on the cheek and joking about who talked the most.

After he and Sir Mozart were back in the apartment, he fed his furry friend and walked to the bathroom. He looked at his face in the mirror and decided he needed a shave, but from his abdomen came the sound of a hungry belly. He rubbed his chin and decided to make breakfast before he shaved.

Just as Dale was filling the kettle with water for hot chocolate, his phone rang. He wondered who could be calling me this early? Then he smiled, it must be Pam.

Dale walked to the bedside table and picked up his phone. When he saw it was E. H., he was surprised to see his call, and he answered, "Hello, E. H. Is everything alright?"

"Yeah, sure; I didn't mean to alarm you. I wanted to invite you to breakfast, church and lunch. We would love to have you join us."

In an instant, the faces of E. H. Denton's family were flashing before Dale's eyes. He tried to think of an excuse, but the words coming out of his mouth did not match his thoughts, "Yes to all three. I can't think of a better way to spend my day. What time should I be there?"

Uplifted E. H. said, "Breakfast will be ready in forty minutes. Can you make it?"

"Yes, I will be there."

"Alright then... Looking forward to seeing you and bring Sir Mozart," said E. H.

"Thanks for inviting us." Dale and E. H. hung up without saying goodbye.

Dale shaved, showered, and dressed in a pair of khaki's, a light blue button-down shirt, and his western boots in record time. He didn't own a tie and hoped it didn't matter.

He had never been to a church, but he knew if it was important to E. H., it was important to him. He grabbed his hat and his keys and rushed out the door.

Stanley was getting out of the ambulance to go inside Edwards Dinner when Dale's Bel Air went by. He wondered if anything was wrong. Dale didn't usually break the speed limit.

Automatically, he looked at his pager to make sure he hadn't missed a call. When he walked in, Cooksey said, "You look puzzled. What's going on?"

"I was wondering why Dale would fly by here," replied Stanley.

"Yeah, I saw his car. I've never seen him in a hurry. Do you think he's headed to the Denton's?" Cooksey asked.

"Could have been," Stanley said jokingly, "Maybe he was late for breakfast."

Cooksey flashed a tooth-filled smile. "Wish we could be that lucky."

After Stanley ordered his breakfast, his mind returned to Dwight's call about the Eight Ball killer. Even though he had not seen the scene himself, Dwight has carefully described it. Something lingered in his brain, and he couldn't reach it.

The criminal was now called the Eight Ball Killer by everyone. Although the sheriff asked for it not to get out, Dwight had leaked it to Stanley and others.

Mentally Stanley believed, the young woman must have gone through hell. Why would someone do that? He has to be sick and evil.

Cooksey brought Stanley's breakfast and stood looking at him. Stanley looked back at him and said, "What?"

Cooksey said, "Just wondering if you had any ideas about the Eight Ball Killer."

"Damn, man! Do you think I'd bet sittin' here if I did?" said Stanley.

Hanging his head, Cooksey said, "Don't guess you would." He walked away.

Stanley would apologize for his harsh reply any other day, but today he continued trying to reach for the lingering question hidden in his brain. He could almost feel it on the tip of his tongue.

All he knew was it had to do with the girl found by the Eagle Creek Bridge and the carved eight ball on her back.

EPISODE 23

Junior Maddox looked at the cold mist hitting the windshield of his custom Jaguar. Tomorrow he would be leaving this mess and headed for Hawaii for three weeks.

He could hardly wait to be somewhere people didn't know him. He was meeting a college buddy. He laughed about his buddy being named Layne Makoa.

Layne was a top-notch attorney in Hawaii, and she was the most beautiful specimen of any woman he had ever seen. They rediscovered each other on Facebook and then Twitter.

In a few months, they were skyping, and when she asked him to come to Hawaii for the holidays, Junior could not believe his luck.

He had to get one thing out of the way. He didn't understand why he felt obliged to visit his father or to tell him where he was going.

Either way, he would be talking to an obnoxious drunk who had become exponentially unbearable in the last year. He didn't know what he had done to deserve how Vernon treated him and knew his father would be annoyed he wasn't coming home on Christmas.

It was late in the afternoon, so Junior drove to Edwards Diner to get food before going to Vernon's house. He ordered three times as much as he needed and two of every dessert on the menu. His father loved sweets.

He stopped by the Food Lion and bought several tea bottles and several Mt. Dews; Vernon loved those too. He bought a case of beer, several boxes of Little Debbie snacks, and a big bag of Snickers.

Junior continued shopping as he picked up a large box of individually wrapped chips, individually wrapped cheeses, several bags of jerky, and several packages of individual fruit cups. He bought plastic cups and plates, paper towels, and toilet tissue.

As he drove to the house where he lived as a child, Junior thought how it did not matter what he bought; his father would never be satisfied.

Junior turned into the driveway, not expecting his father to be at home. Vernon's truck and the sheriff's car were in the driveway, so he pulled on the grass if his father had to leave quickly.

He took the food from Edward's in first, sat it on the table, and walked back to the car two more times to get the things he had purchased. After he put everything away, he went into the living room and called, "Vernon, are you home?"

The commode flushed, and the bathroom door opened. Vernon came out and looked at his son and said, "Didn't expect you today."

Junior blinked his eyes a couple of times as if he couldn't believe what he saw or heard. Vernon used no curse words. He stood in front of Junior with his uniform pressed, freshly shaven, and what appeared to be a new haircut.

"Brought you some food, Dad." It was rare for Junior to call his father "Dad," and he didn't understand why he said it."

"Yeah, I smell it from here. It's a little earlier than I usually eat, but I am hungry. You gonna join me?"

What in the hell is going on? Am I in some type of weird alternate world? Is this man an imposter? Thoughts were going through Junior's brain like a runaway train as he said, "Ahh, ahh, yeah, I'm hungry too."

Junior followed Vernon into the kitchen, and his father began taking utensils from a drawer and placing them on the table. Then Vernon opened the refrigerator and looked at his choices; Mt. Dew, tea, and beer. He reached for a Mt. Dew and tuned to Junior, "What do you want?"

He wants something big this time, thought Junior. "I'll have some tea."

Vernon took a gallon of tea and then went to the cabinet for a glass. Then he put ice in his glass and turned to Junior and said, "This is a lot of food."

Junior couldn't take it anymore and said, "Ok, Vernon, what's up with you? I haven't seen you like this since Ppp...in a long time."

"Why in the hell were you going to mention Pearl? You damn well know I didn't care anything about that woman. You need to shut the hell up." Vernon put the glass down on the table so hard some of the ice bounced out, and then he started laughing as Junior glared at this Vernon. But, when Vernon stopped laughing, he said in an angry voice, "Sit down, Junior."

With Vernon back in character, Junior began telling him what was on each plate and about the desserts. He then added I put other snacks in the cabinet and some cheese in the refrigerator.

Junior sat down and poured tea into his glass. He reached for one of the bags and opened it. Each plate was huge, and he wondered if he could eat it all.

Vernon spoke, "You wanna share your plate, Son? I want to save room for some dessert." He looked at the shock on his son's face and gave him a yellowed, toothy grin.

He's gone again. Maybe he is on drugs. As Junior was thinking how weird his father was, Vernon got up from the table and retrieved two plates, real plates...not paper ones. He said, "You take what you want, and I'll take the rest. You can have those lima beans; they give me gas."

"Ok, Vernon, what are you up to? You have never been nice to me. What's going on?"

Smiling, Vernon said, "Been thinking about retiring and catching up on fishin' and huntin' or maybe go to see the Grand Canyon; always wanted to see it.

Junior took out the food he wanted and pushed the take-out plate towards his father. He squinted at Vernon and placed his index finger firmly across his lips as if to hold the words. Vernon looked at him and then continued taking the rest of the food from the diner container and placing it on his plate. "Did you want a piece of this cornbread?"

Ok, old man. I'll play your game and see where it takes us, Junior thought and then said, "You should take a trip to Las Vegas, and from there you can take a helicopter trip or a bus trip to The Grand Canyon, Death Valley, and Hoover Dam. You can even take a trip out to Hollywood."

Vernon listened intently, and when Junior stopped talking, he asked, "Does any of those places around there look like the western movies?"

"Yes, it does. You can visit Montana, Wyoming, Colorado, and New Mexico during late spring or early summer. I have heard of tours that visit sites where movies have been made, including TV towns and museums.

During the same time, the snow on the mountains is something to see, and the wildlife is remarkable in Yellowstone National Park," Junior said, forgetting he was talking to his father and having the first conversation of their lives. "I could help you plan a trip, Dad. You might want to plan on a three- or four-week trip. You could see so much, and you may not ever want to come home. It is beautiful county."

"Oh yeah, I heard there are also train tours you can take to those places. You can go right across the whole USA."

Junior looked at Vernon and realized his father finished his meal, had his elbows on the table, and looked at him like a real father or what he imagined a real father would be.

"You staying the night, Junior?" Vernon asked.

Nervously, Junior said, "I could. Do I still have clothes in my room?" He was afraid the mood would disappear.

"I've never removed anything from your room, so any clothes you brought here should still be here. I'd like it if you would stay...even if you want to leave early in the morning. I need to go into work about six in the morning anyway."

"Yeah, I'll stay. I could try to find you a vacation deal for seeing the Grand Canyon if you want me to."

"I would like for us to go together, Junior." Vernon bit his lip and scratched his head, and said, "Would you go with me?

Junior almost choked on his dessert and willed his eyes not to well with tears. How can this be the Vernon Maddox I've always known? Why such a change? Is he dying? "If you mean it, Vernon, I would like to go," he said as he cleared his brain and made a fake cough while trying to hide his emotions. Emotions he never thought he would have concerning his father.

EPISODE 24

It was five minutes to midnight, and all the church members were gathering in large, circular patterns in the church's recreation room.

The Denton's and the Webb's made their circle, including Dale, Stanley, and Pam. Soon all began the countdown to the New Year.... ten, nine, eight, seven, six, five, four, three, two, one.

On one, everyone was blowing their paper horns, beating their tambourines, or shaking their bells as someone pulled the net away, so all sizes of balloons fell upon the crowd below.

Dale could see people hugging and couples kissing while the children were jumping up and down, yelling Happy New Year.

To Dale, it looked like a choreographed event. Someone told him it was a tradition in the church, but he thought, *wouldn't it be nice if all humans were purposed to live, love, and exist in harmony.*

Soon everyone gathered their family with their coats on and empty dishes in hand. After most people left, a few stayed to clean. E. H. was one of them, so Dale, Stanley, and Pam stayed also. The three friends were grateful to be celebrating with all the good people of the church.

Since Dale had driven, he took Pam home first. When Dale stopped in her driveway, she leaned in and kissed Dale's cheek. Before exiting the vehicle, she turned to Stanley and blew him a kiss.

Both men watched as she walked to her door, unlocked it, and went in. Neither Dale nor Stanley had any idea sometime in the future, Pam would leave, and they would never see her again.

EPISODE 25

When Dale arrived home after the New Year's Eve party, he was exhausted, but he could not sleep. He got out of bed turned on the television. He and Sir Mozart watched celebrations around the world until daylight.

Dale had a strange feeling he couldn't shake, and the only thing he could think to blame was the grey letter. He read it several times before he took it to the kitchen and struck a match. It had said for him to be ready to embark on August 4th, the anniversary of his seventh and last mission year.

He watched the letter burn. He did not know if it was ordinary to receive this information while on a mission, especially since he received the same information while at the Yucca, Nevada Base.

He did not know if he would receive more calls which would lead him to another letter. He had to decide what to do about the instructions. He needed to talk to his handler, Inrun52.

He had not received any written message while he and Rex were in South American, so Dale wanted to know if it was real or if someone had found out he was on the mission to destroy a large part of the North Carolina cartel.

Dale spent the first few days of the year working on a new addition to Rodney's garage. Since Dale had been there, Rodney Medlin's business had grown. Repairs and older model car restoration had increased one hundred percent over the last four months.

Rodney had many connections, and from time to time, someone would tell him about an old car they believed needed rescuing. Parked in the garage was a blue and white '56 Fairlane.

Dale began by taking the motor out. Since he was alone, it was not as easy, but he was in no hurry. He was trying to keep his mind occupied.

When he was taking a break, he was thinking about Rodney and his locked art room. Was he correct? No one went into the room but Rodney.

Dale often heard him banging and pounding on metal. He could hear cracking and sparking when Rodney used the welding machine and smelled the metal's odor reaching the melting point.

Since he had to use the forklift, Rodney Medlin couldn't hide the shipments of sheets of aluminum and other metals before they entered the art garage.

When Dale went to work, Rodney told him three things; he would pay Dale an honest wage for his work, Dale could set his hours, and he was not to ask any questions unless it was about the automobile he was repairing.

Dale had not minded the rules, but he became more curious about the secrete art garage every day. He had seen several of the metal sculptures Rodney brought out and realized he had a unique talent.

It was usually art made out of all kinds of car parts, gears, and pieces of metal sheets. There were metal trees, stars, suns, flowers, and an array of animals.

Dale also wondered about the automobiles, campers, vans, and other vehicles which came into the garage in the middle of the night. When they arrived, it was always after regular working hours. Dale didn't understand what the vehicles had to do with Rodney's art projects.

Dale sat on an upside-down bucket in the opened garage door area, eating a pocket pizza and drinking a Dr. Pepper while thinking about the secrete garage. He had seen Rodney remove the key from an unusual place once.

He knew Rodney kept the primary key with him, but Rodney had misplaced his keys one day and was in a hurry. Dale had looked around to reach for a wrench from the workbench and saw Rodney. He had quickly turned his head, so Rodney didn't notice.

He began thinking, what would it hurt? Rodney won't be back until Sunday. He will never know.

Dale walked to the spot where Rodney had removed the extra key. Rodney had a collection of water pistols along the wall. They all hung under a nail below an old neon sign which said, Shoot em up."

There were about 50 of them, but there was one black plastic gun. Dale took the gun from the nail and turned it over. Half of the grip was missing on the backside. Dale shook it, and the secrete garage key fell out. He quickly opened the door.

What Dale saw amazed and shocked him. A white van was in the shop, and all the doors were off. Three of the doors had secreted compartments already in place.

He looked in the van, and there was a dummy top to the van which Rodney had started. When finished, Dale could see that it could hold drugs or money and look like any other top to any van.

Dale quickly broke into a sweat. He believed Rodney was one of the good guys, but he was also doing things to help the bad guys succeed in transporting whatever they could fit in the created hidden spaces.

He looked under another van and saw a larger gas tank than it was supposed to be and guessed it probably had a small chamber.

Dale stopped in his tracks when he saw a wooden sign with metal letters that said, 'Mad Dog.' "What the hell," he said out loud.

Dale heard a noise. He panicked and peered out the door but saw no one. He quickly went out, locked the door, and put the key back in its hiding place.

He heard another noise and whipped around. His heart felt as if it was about to explode, and then he saw her...that darn albino cat.

He felt like throwing a wrench at her, but instead, he called her up to the apartment and gave her milk. She stretched out on the sofa and fell asleep as Dale looked enviously at her.

He just wanted to fall asleep, too, but there was no way it would happen for a while. When he went to the bathroom, he noticed he was whiter than the cat.

Dale had to get out of the garage to wake up the sleeping Sir Mozart and headed for Webb's Mill.

When they arrived, there was no one else there. Dale got out of the truck, lifted the dog out, and walked down the rock-filled path and to the riverbank. He sat on the same rock as he had the first time when the Martins thought he was the ghost of their dead son, Stephen.

Dale listened to the water and watched Sir Mozart wander around while contemplating what he would do about what he saw in Rodney Medlin's art garage.

EPISODE 26

It was an abnormally warm January day as Vernon sat at his desk wondering when his detectives would find a break in the Eight Ball murders. He had made up his mind on New Year's Eve; after he solved the case, he would retire.

He would take a portion of the money he had saved and travel to the United States. He had no desire to go outside of the country. There were so many places he wanted to see.

Vernon had found a television channel that constantly showed places in the United States which were beautiful and inviting.

Every time he watched one of the programs, he wanted to pack up and hit the road. He knew what Junior said, but he did not expect him to travel across the country with his father.

Vernon knew it would end as a disaster. They would never be able to agree on anything.

Vernon took a picture of his little girl, Verna, from his billfold and looked at it. Pearl had sent a new one on his birthday. To him, it meant Pearl still thought of him.

At that moment, he made up his mind he would do everything in his power to find Pearl and Verna. They were the people he would take with him to discover the United States; his family.

Sheriff Maddox put the picture back in his billfold, got up from his chair, and opened his blinds. He could see Detective Cain and Detective Perez standing in front of the whiteboard where there were pictures of the Eight Ball case. They were arguing.

Vernon opened the door, pointed, and said, "You two get the hell in here."

The detectives looked at each other and walked towards the Sheriff's office. Vernon went behind his desk when they got near the door, but he did not sit down.

When Detectives Cain and Perez came into his office, they stood in attention as if they were in front of a military general. They stood waiting for whatever Vernon was going to hand them.

"Damn it, sit down."

At the same time, the two said, "Yes, Sir." They quickly sat in the hard-bottom chairs there since the sheriff's office began many years before.

"What are you two arguing about? Don't you have enough work to do?" Vernon asked.

Detective Cain spoke up, saying, "Sir, Detective Perez wants to go undercover and try to flush out the Eight Ball killer."

Before Vernon could speak, Detective Perez slid to the front of her chair and said, "Sir, I was undercover for two years when I worked in Miami, and I am sure I could be of great help here."

Vernon Maddox sat down and looked at the two for a full minute before he spoke. The silence made the two anxious as they were expecting an attack filled with curse words. "Tell me about your ideas, Perez."

"Well, Sir. I-I-I considered hanging out with the other working girls on the corner of Main and South Street?"

Vernon's crooked smile went across his face in a flash. "No."

"But, Sir…."

"I said, no, Perez. I will not risk the life of an officer, and it would be a poor use of your detective skills."

The two detectives looked at each other with puzzlement. Sheriff Maddox had insinuated Perez had skills. Where was the sheriff they knew and did not love?

Vernon realized he sounded soft and quickly corrected the notion. "Detective Perez, what makes you think the killer would be picking up girls on the corner of Main and South Street.

You two do realize there have been six other murders, and only two of those were hookers. The others, including the one near Stonehope, were women who were either in a mall parking lot or at a convenient store."

"Yes, Sir," Perez replied.

"Detective Cain, tell me all the facts you have on the Eight Ball murders and tell me who the hell let everyone in five counties know these women had an eight ball on their backs?"

"Sheriff," said Cain, "No one knows who leaked the info, but we have worked with the other counties and have a person of interest."

Vernon threw his head back and laughed. "You have been watching too much TV. What does this person of interest look like?"

"He drives a black 2007 ford truck and wears a mask that looks like the president," Cain said and waited for Vernon to yell at him.

"I've already been informed of those facts by Wilson County. Do you have anything else?"

"No, Sir." Said, Detective Cain. Detective Perez was shaking her head, indicating they did not have any information.

"You two better rethink your plans. The murderer killed seven women in five counties in one month. It has been six weeks since any murder like the Eight Ball MO has been reported anywhere in North Carolina. I know you have been working with the task force in the other counties and have been reporting the findings to me.

I want you to tell me again about the profile and any information you and others have found. Start from the beginning, Jim."

"Yes, Sir, the profiler believes the person is a white male in his late forties, and he has some training in medicine. He also thinks this man is primarily a loner, and he has some sort of power over the people he works with or for.

So far, he picks his victims late at night or early morning when few people are around. We believe he is approximately six feet tall and thin from the video footage of the convenience stores and one outside the mall in Wilson County.

In both videos, he has on the mask of the president and some purple gloves. He is also dressed in black and has his hoody pulled up, making it impossible to see his hair. We do not know for sure if he is a white man."

When Detective Cain paused, Perez took over. Sheriff, in both videos, the perp walks up to the women as they are opening their car door. It appears he puts a cloth on their face, and they become limp.

Since the killer parks beside each vehicle, it is easy for him to put the woman in his truck bed. So far, the women he picks are small in stature. He gets into the truck and drives away. The convenience store video shows his tag covered with what we think is duct tape.

When Perez stopped talking, Sheriff Maddox asked, "Is there anything on any of the bodies to show where he might be taking them?"

Perez nods to her partner, and Cain says, "The medical examiners say nothing is showing they were outdoors except the grasses or weeds which were at the dumpsite.

There are bruises and burns on their wrist and legs as if tied. There were dog hairs on one of the bodies, but they were from the victim's dog."

"What about the cloth the victim uses?" Vernon asked.

"The medical examiners say it appears to be some type of gauze used in most emergency rooms," answered Perez.

Vernon's office became quiet while the detectives and the sheriff stared at each other. Vernon broke the silence saying, "Has the FBI had any similar cases in the past?"

Cain said, "No, Sir. Their agent said they went back twenty years and searched every database they have."

"What are they saying about the time-lapse. It has been weeks since the last murder?" Vernon asked.

Perez spoke first, "They don't know, Sheriff. It is a puzzle to them. They did say it could mean it was someone a lot of people knew, and he is smart enough to lay low for a while."

Sheriff Maddox stood up and said, "Thank you. Keep me informed on anything new you hear, and Perez, don't put yourself at risk. Understand?"

"Yes, Sir." Vernon then walked out of the room and out of the station leaving the two detectives wondering why he did not bombard them with curse words.

EPISODE 27

Dale and Rodney had been busy in the garage since Rodney returned from his vacation in January. It seemed to Dale half the population of Blackstone County had been to the garage for repairs.

Dale didn't think about the word was getting around; <u>he</u> was the best mechanic in the area. Even women came with their cars because they felt Dale would not take advantage of their lack of knowledge concerning car repairs.

He and Rodney both were staying busy, and Rodney was also working in his art garage many nights.

Since Dale visited the 'art garage,' he began noticing the people who were allowed inside. Most he did not recognize. However, there was one he did remember: Junior Maddox, the son of the sheriff.

Dale wished he had never gone into the garage. He was disappointed in Rodney, and sometimes it was hard not to show it.

"Hey, Rodney, when I finish this car, I'm going to call it a day," Dale said.

"Sure, Dale, you have been working a lot of hours the past few weeks. Go out and have a little fun."

As Dale was washing the grease from his hands, he saw Rodney taking his keys out of his pocket and then unlocked the art garage. Dale stiffened and rushed to get to his apartment. He did not want to think of anything but having a good time.

After he showered and shaved, Dale sat in the reclining chair and turned on the television to watch the news. He took a swallow of his iced tea and then blew out a big breath of air.

He closed his eyes and listened as he willed his body and mind out of the tense state it had been in for weeks. In a few minutes, he fell asleep.

Dale began to dream. He was in an old house surrounded by woods. He heard someone crying; it was Pam. He ran into a room in the house and saw a black figure standing on a billiard table throwing balls at her. There was a whole bucket of eight balls, and the black figure laughed every time he hit Pam with a ball.

He knew that laugh, and it was…Dale woke up saying no, no, no and in his mind, he heard music…He shook his head and realized it was his phone…." Hello."

"Sorry, Dale," Pam said, "I didn't mean to wake you."

"It's OK, Pam. I guess I fell asleep watching the news. We have been busy at the garage lately, and I guess it caught up with me. What's up?"

"Nothing; I am just checking on you. I haven't seen or heard from you in a couple of weeks. There is a good movie playing in Raleigh this weekend. I was wondering if you wanted to go see it."

"It looks like I will be working Saturday. Can we go to the late one?"

"Yes. That's what I had in mind. I have to work too. We can try to make the ten o'clock one."

"Yeah, the ten o'clock movie will be good. I need a break, so what time do you want me to pick you up?"

"I'm taking a change of clothes to work so you can pick me up there at eight. We can stop for a pizza before the movie."

"Good idea. It's been a while since we ate pizza. I'll pick you up at eight. Thanks for calling, Pam. See you Saturday night. Bye." Dale had no idea it was a Valentin's Day celebration.

Pam spoke softly and said, "Bye, Dale."

As soon as the call ended, he called Stanley. When Stanley answered, he said, "Are you home or working?"

Stanley said, "I am off until five tomorrow morning. Come on over. I have some special hot chocolate ready."

"I'll stop at Simon's Food Bar, get burgers, and be right over," Dale said. He was relieved Stanley was home. They needed to talk.

EPISODE 28

E. H. drove to the flower shop and then to the church. Memories of the past flowed like a river through his brain. If he had been sitting across from someone, they would have seen smiles, tears, anger, laughter, crying, and sorrow...lots of heartaches.

Usually, he did not allow himself to go through so many memories. He would try to restrain from thinking about Sarah for days, and then he would be filled with guilt because he believed he was betraying his wife.

He sat in the car with the roses lying on the seat beside him. He sobbed out loud and asked God why again and again.

Then he yelled at God for taking a good woman. After all that, he asked God for forgiveness and apologizes for questioning God's wisdom.

With his mental energy spent, he picked up the roses, opened the door, and got out. He thought *it smells like it is going to snow.*

E. H. shivered as he remembered his father and his grandfather saying the same thing. *Maybe it is a Denton trait*, he thought.

It was almost midday, and the temperature only slightly above freezing. E. H. walked to his wife's grave and talked to her just like he did at night when everyone else was asleep, and they were alone. He also cried.

Before he left, he laid the roses down and said to his wife, "It is going to snow, Honey, and it's going to be a big one. I wish you were here."

EPISODE 29

During Katherine's shift, she had seen three people die. One was very old and had lived a good life. His family gathered around him until his last breath.

They had spent his final hours telling stories of his life and talking about, as children, they learned a lot from him.

Two of his sons told him about things they had done which they had never told their father. Everyone laughed, and the dying man smiled. Katherine had been in and out of the room and could not help but be emotional.

When her patient died, she knew he was happy right up until the last second; and would be forever. She had to believe.

The following person who died was a young man of nineteen. He had drunk himself into a stupor soon after snorting heroin. When he began throwing up and twitching with cramps, his under-aged friends became afraid.

While they were trying to decide what to do, the young man's heart stopped. They called 911 and left the house before the paramedics arrived. They were successful in restarting his heart, but the young man was brain dead.

His family decided to pull the plug at 6:32 AM, the same time he was born.

Another person to expire was an older woman who did not have heat. Her neighbors found her late morning, barely breathing. Her body, frozen beyond what the doctors could do for her.

She had no family or friends. None of her neighbors would stay, so Katherine had held her hand until the last. Even though the woman never regained consciousness, Katherine hated to see people die alone.

Overdoses also caused the deaths which bothered her most. A sixteen-year-old girl and her eighteen-year-old boyfriend had celebrated Valentine's Day by purchasing what they believed to be cocaine.

However, the person selling the drugs sold them a small portion of heroin mixed with non-pharmaceutical Fentanyl. They went into seizures and died almost instantly. Their friends called 911, but they were DOA at the site.

At lunchtime, she went to the desk to sign out for a few minutes and found a dozen red roses from Larry. She smiled because she knew E. H. would be taking the chocolate cake she had baked to the fire department. It was a tradition her mother-in-law kept, and Katherine wanted to continue it.

Mama Sarah told Katherine the men who worked at the fire department were like family to Larry, and they all enjoyed the cake.

Katherine knew the sweetest Valentine would be when she and Larry were home and alone. It helped her make it through the day.

Martin and Dorothy Webb cooked their favorite meal together for Valentine's Day. They sat at the table discussing the events of recent months, which included Dale Weaver's arrival and how much he looked like Stephen.

They believed they knew why but had not mentioned it to E. H. They decided to do so soon.

EPISODE 30

Earlier in the day, Sheriff Vernon Maddox asked Detective Perez to buy him three roses and put them in his patrol car. She assured him it was his secrete. He had smiled at her.

Later, Vernon took the three roses to the river bridge and dropped in two for Pearl and one for Verna, got into his car, and went back to the office.

EPISODE 31

Dale pulled into the parking lot of Edwards Diner and waited. It was snowing, and there was about an inch on the ground. The snow was not sticking to the roads, but the prediction was for heavy snow, later on, accumulating on all surfaces.

It is his first snow. He was amazed at the beauty and the way the snow fell on his skin and immediately melted.

While driving to the diner, Dale meditated on the beauty of the snow as it hit his windshield. To him, some of the snowflakes looked like little creatures trying to avoid the collision. He smiled and thought, *this moment is worth whatever this mission is going to be.*

He pulled into the diner parking lot and stopped. Pam was at the door before he realized it. When she got into the car, she was still in her uniform. She said, "Turn on the heat. I'm freezing."

Dale laughed and said, "You don't like the snow?"

"Yes, yes, yes. I love it, but I want to be warm while I'm looking at it. A few minutes ago, there was an announcement on the radio saying we might get seven or eight inches. I guess our movie trip is off."

Dale could not imagine how all these tiny flakes could fall and make seven inches of snow. "Yeah, we might get to Raleigh, but we might have to stay." He said.

"Let's go to my house. I have a couple of frozen pizzas, some beer, and later we can go out and throw snowballs at each other. Then we can go back in and have hot chocolate."

"It was what Jimmy and I used to do." Pam was talking as fast as she could. She was very excited, but when Jimmy's name came out of her mouth, she sat quiet and stiff.

Dale knew she had lost a son named Jimmy, but he didn't know anymore. He saw the immediate change in Pam and tried to help. "Pam, I would love to do it all."

He wanted to tell her he had never seen snow and never made a snowball, but he was supposed to be from Canada, and it would be a giant red flag. So, he just said, "I've never thrown a snowball at anyone. Does it hurt?"

She looked at him with disbelief and said, "Don't be fooling me. You were a kid where there was lots of snow. If you think you are going to sneak up on me, you have another thought coming."

Laughing it off, Dale said, "We'll see who wins. The loser has to pay for our next night out."

Pam punched him in the arm as hard as she could and said, "I ain't a prissy girl. I'm going to win big time, and I'll pick the most expensive place I can find with the biggest steak."

They both were laughing when they pulled up in front of Pam's place. The snow was coming down in big flakes, and the wind was blowing. They both got out of the car and ran to the door. Pam had a sweater on, and her whole body was shaking.

Dale took the key and opened the door, and they both rushed into the house. Pam slipped her shoes off and told Dale to wait at the door. She brought back a large bath towel and put it on the floor. Put your shows there so I won't have a puddle at the door.

Dale turned on the TV while Pam took a frozen pizza out of the freezer. She added more cheese, black olives, and bacon bits before she put it in the oven. She got two beers and sat down beside Dale on the couch.

"Pam, now they are saying we might get as much as ten or eleven inches of snow. Maybe I'd better go on home."

She looked at Dale like he was crazy and said, "No way are you going to chicken out. I'm going to burst your butt with snowballs. Besides, I don't want to eat all the pizza alone.

If you can't get home, I'll give you blankets and a pillow so you can sleep on the couch. It is the heaviest snow we've had in a long time, and we ain't going to waste it."

Dale looked at Pam's happy face and was delighted he had a great friend like her. "What do you want to watch?"

"Do you like old westerns?" Pam asked.

He had seen a few westerns, but he mainly watched them for the scenery, so he said, "A few. But it sounds perfect. What do you have?"

Pam walked to the cabinet beside the TV and opened the door. She took out Dancing with Wolves and said, "This is perfect."

Dale felt conflicted about asking Pam the question he had on his mind, but he thought she might have heard someone say something at the restaurant that could help.

When she sat down on the couch, he said, "Pam, can we talk a few minutes. I've heard a few things that have me concerned."

"What kind of things?" She asked.

"I've heard a few people talking about Mad Dog lately. Do you know who he is and what he does? The tone went off on Pam's oven, and she said, "Pizza's ready. We'll talk while we eat."

Dale sat at the table while Pam gathered everything needed. They both took a big bite out of their slice of pizza. "Umm. This is the best pizza I've ever eaten," said Dale.

Pam gave him thumbs up. She drank part of her beer and asked, "Why do you want to know about Mad Dog?"

"I've heard about all the drugs going up and down 95 Highway, and some say Blackstone County is a transitional point," replied Dale.

"I believe it is true. Have you been out to the exit of the 95 called Gold Dust?"

"Yes, I rode out there one day and ate at one of the restaurants. There are also three large motels out there. It looks like a lot of rooms for people to stay.

There seems to be no attraction for pulling people from the highway. But I did notice a few women walking around in attire I would call questionable."

"Pam laughed and said, "I hear those girls make a lot of money."

Dale looked at Pam with a blank face. He wasn't in a kidding mood.

When Pam saw the seriousness of Dale's face, she said, "Ok. I've heard Gold Dust is the center of the drug route between Florida and the northern states.

Most everyone around here knows it is a drug and cash exchange out there. Some say a drug cartel owns all the businesses even though they have local people running them.

"Why hasn't someone stopped it? Dale asked.

Pam shrugged her shoulders and said, "Same reason all over the world; money."

"Is this Mad Dog running this area?"

"It is what most people think, but I wonder if he isn't working for someone much more important."

"Do you think the dead girl at Eagle Creek Bridge has anything to do with the drug trafficking?" asked Dale.

"I don't think so. She was the seventh of the Eight Ball murderer." Pam said.

Dale's dream of a man throwing eight balls at Pam seared across his mind. He turned to her and said, "What did you say?"

"I said the Eight Ball murderer. He has killed seven women."

"Where did you hear he was called the Eight Ball murderer?" Dale quickly asked.

"A couple of the deputies were talking about it at the restaurant the other day. They said the murderer carves a circle in their backs and put the number eight in the circle."

Dale didn't move. He just kept looking at Pam across the table. He was thinking, Should I tell her about the dream? But he said, "I have not heard that."

His face showed seriousness as he said, "Pam, you need to be more careful when you go out." There was no way he was going to try to explain.

When they finished eating, he excused himself and went into the bathroom. Dale propped himself on the sink and looked into the mirror.

Dale was afraid for Pam, and he did not know what to do. He decided to talk to Stanley. He relieved himself, washed his hands, and walked out of the bathroom.

Dale didn't know Pam was waiting for him with a huge snowball. When it hit him in the chest, Pam ran back out the front door in her bare feet and returned with another snowball. Still, in shock with the first one, he froze as she smashed snow in his face.

He pushed Pam away; she slipped on the wet snow and fell to the floor laughing so hard she couldn't get up. She began rolling around on the wet floor, laughing so hard she looked bizarre. His education had not prepared him for this; snowballs and rolling on the floor laughing.

Pam stopped laughing, got up from the floor, and stood in front of what she thought was an angry Dale. "Guess you don't like being ambushed with snowballs."

Dale looked at Pam's damp hair and then down at her bare red feet. The front door was still open, and the room was chilly.

He picked her up and threw her over his shoulder, and walked out to the front yard. Four or five inches of snow lay on the ground. She was kicking and laughing and yelling, "No."

He laid her in the snow and rolled her over and over. They both were laughing when he again picked her up and put her on his shoulder. She went limp, and he thought he had hurt her.

He rushed into the apartment, lay her on the couch, and put the multicolored afghan on her. She did not move. He shook her.

All of a sudden, she became alive with snow in both hands. She reached into the back of Dale's shirt and let go of the wet snow. She yelled, "Happy Valentine's Day.

Dale stood up and said, "What?" He took his shirttail out and tried to shake out the snow, but it was primarily cold water. He looked at Pam lying on the couch, trying not to laugh. "You little troublemaker. I'll fix you.

He began to tickle Pam. She rolled onto the floor to try to get away, but he was relentless. She reached into his jeans pant leg and began pulling his leg hairs.

"What the hell?" He jumped away and stood there looking at her.

She looked like a wet kitten. Dale took a couple of more steps backward and said, "Seriously, Pam. You better get some dry clothes on."

He reached for her hand and helped her up. She smiled as she wiped her wet hair from her face. Dale was thinking, this must be what it feels like to have a little sister.

Pam was thinking, and I wish you would take my wet clothes off and take me to the shower. She could see by Dale's expression he was thinking something different.

"Sure. After you get out, we can watch the movie you picked out." Dale was missing all the signs of Pam's passion.

While he was cleaning the kitchen, he considered what Pam said about Valentine's Day. He had seen the advertisements on the TV but did not know it was such a big thing.

Dale just thought it was a ploy for people to buy flowers, cards, or candy. He decided to let it go and ask Stanley later.

After the movie, Dale and Pam put on their coats and walked out to the edge of the street. The light from the streetlamp made the snow glisten on the landscape.

Dale reflected on how the snow changes everything and seems to make it all new and fresh. He wished it could make all the bad things go away, but he knew better.

When they came back in, Pam brought a pillow and blankets for the couch. He did not see the streaks where her tears slid down her face. He spent the night and slept very well, but Pam's body and sadness did not allow her to do so.

 The following weekend she got the big steak at the most excellent restaurant in Raleigh. However, she was still hurt and confused. She had dressed in her sexiest dress made several sexy gestures and comments while on the way. She had even tried to kiss him on the mouth when he took her home.

Not understanding, Dale had gently pushed her back and kissed her on her forehead. She felt rejected and demoralized. She would not let him see the hurt, so she decided not to respond to him at all.

EPISODE 32

Vernon Maddox sat in his office armed with his black coffee watching his officers come and go. He had just talked to the FBI contact about the Eight Ball Killer. There had been no more murders with the same MO.

Vernon knew his main thought should not be his delayed retirement but what was going on in Blackstone County. He picked up the phone and asked Detective Cain and Perez to come in and talk with him. Cain reported they would be there in about twenty minutes.

Vernon nursed his coffee and had the urge to open his bottom desk drawer and add a little bourbon. The fight was not as bad as it used to be. Over the last few weeks, he had decided he was not an alcoholic. He didn't have any problem not drinking.

He knew everyone was talking. Not because he drank at the office but because he had almost stopped drinking and his personality had calmed to make him a damn good boss. He smiled at himself and mentally said, *I believe Pearl will be proud of me.*

There was a tap on the door. Vernon looked up and saw Perez and Cain. He motioned for them to come in. "Take a seat. I want to run something by you." Vernon said.

None of the people in the Blackstone County Sheriff's Department could understand what had happened to Vernon Maddox. His personality seemed to have had changed overnight. Everyone was waiting for the other shoe to drop.

"Sure," said Detective Perez.

The Sheriff was rolling a pencil between his fingers as he looked at the two officers. They looked anxious, so he said, "I know both of you have been working with the FBI and the profiler trying to catch the Eight Ball Killer.

It's good there have not been any more murders, and for that very reason, it seems every lead is a dead end. You have kept me up to date, and I appreciate all the hours you put into the investigation.

The two detectives looked at each other. It was hard to get used to the gentle and kinder man. Cain spoke up. "We were hoping you were going to tell us something changed, and we had more clues."

"No. But I do have something I want you to do for me. It can go no further than this office." Vernon said.

"The two looked at each other again, and Perez looked the sheriff in the eyes and said, "Sir, I do not believe you will find two detectives who are as straight as we are." Cain was unconsciously shaking his head up and down. Perez added, "You can trust us."

"Vernon waited a few seconds before he spoke. He cleared his throat and said, "I have two people in mind, and I have not heard you say anything about either one of them. They both fit part of the profile.

"We probably know at least one of the people. Is it Dwight Gacy?"

"Yes. Gacy is one. The other is Rodney Medlin. I don't know if he had any medical training, but I've seen some of his carvings of wood, and he also does art in metal."

"We looked at Dwight Gacy, and he had an alibi for the night of the one near Stonehope, and his buddy confirmed it. We will see what we can find out about Rodney Medlin," said Detective Cain.

Vernon stood and thanked the two for their work and told them to take a couple of days off as soon as they checked on Rodney Medlin. He offered them his hand. They shook hands and left.

Vernon opened his drawer and poured two fingers of bourbon into his coffee cup. He just needed to calm his nerves. He believed he was not an alcoholic and wanted to be the best man he could be for Pearl and their daughter.

With these thoughts, he poured the bourdon into the trash can and set his cup aside.

EPISODE 33

It was an unusual Saturday morning for the Denton's; everyone was home for the day. It was a little past five, and E. H. was sitting at the table drinking coffee.

He had already made biscuits, cooked fatback, and made hot chocolate for Skylar and Jordan. He knew it would be a while before the others woke up, so he enjoyed the noise of the rain hitting against the window. It had been windy and raining for two days, but the weather report said it would be ending late afternoon.

Ratchet began to bark, and E. H. thought he heard a car door, so he got up and pulled the kitchen curtain back. It was still dark, but the area light showed Dale Weaver's truck. E. H. dropped the curtain and headed to the door just as Dale knocked.

He opened it, expecting Dale's usual smile and happy demeanor. There was no happy smile, and the young man looked as if he had lost his best friend. E. H. would discover Dale's thinking was of a 'lost friend.'

"Good morning, Dale. You are out early," E. H. said.

"I need some help E. H. I have a big problem, and I don't understand what happened," Dale replied.

"Sit down, son," said E. H. as he poured the hot water in Dale's cup and handed him the hot chocolate mix. "What's going on?

Dale was shaking his head back and forth before he began to speak. Dale's lips pressed together lightly as he looked into his cup.

He said, "It's about Pam. She is upset with me, and I do not know what I did. I asked her what was wrong, but she just shrugged her shoulders." Dale said as he looked questioningly at E. H.

"I think it was the night of the snow. We were going to Raleigh for a movie and a meal, but I was afraid we would get stuck there if there was too much snow. Pam asked me to her house for frozen pizza and beer.

After the pizza, I excused myself, and when I came out of the restroom, she threw a snowball which hit me in the chest. She then ran outside in her bare feet, got more snow, and smashed it in my face."

Dale stopped talking and looked at E. H with a puzzled look. More than once, E. H. noticed how Pam acted around in the last few months. It was apparent she was in love with him

"What happened next?" E. H asked.

"She fell to the floor and was rolling around in the melted snow laughing hysterically. In an instant, she got up and asked me if I liked snowball fights.

Dale continued, "I picked her up, took her to the deepest snow in the yard, and rolled her over and over. she was laughing and called me silly names."

Dale took a sip of his hot chocolate and continued, "I put her on my shoulder, she suddenly went limp, and I thought I had hurt her.

I took her back into the house, lay her on the sofa, and covered her with a blanket."

"What then?" asked E. H.

"She did not respond, so I leaned over her and shook her gently. She started laughing and put two handfuls of snow under my shirt. I called her a little troublemaker and started tickling her." Dale looked at E. H. as if he were a little boy who was in trouble and didn't understand why.

E. H. could see all the questions on Dale's face and thought to himself, and I wonder if he doesn't know Pam is in love with him. How could he not know? Then he asked Dale, "What happened next?"

Dale said, "Next? It was bizarre. She fell onto the floor again and reached up my pants, and pulled the hairs on my leg. Strange, right? I then stepped back and told her to get up and put some dry clothes on. I didn't want her to get sick. She looked like a wet cat."

E. H. was smiling when he asked, "What did she do then?"

"She just stood there with a strange look on her face until I told her we would watch a movie after she got out of the shower."

"So, she took a shower?" E. H. asked.

Dale looked at him as if he could not believe E. H. had asked the question. "Yes, she took a shower, and we watched the movie. Afterward, we walked around outside. She asked me to stay and brought me a pillow and a blanket, but she had the same strange look on her face."

Dale took a deep breath and said, "That's it." However, Dale continued, "In the morning, I left. She barely spoke to me, and I don't understand why. She still was acting weird. She's been acting like that for weeks. What do you think?"

"How do you feel about Pam? E. H. asked.

Baffled, Dale said, "What do you mean?"

E. H. tried another approach, "Do you have feelings for Pam?"

Dale smiled and said, "Of course I do. She is like the little sister I never had. Which is what I was thinking when she was playing in the snow."

"Oh. Yep, you are in a big mess." E. H. said.

Bewildered, Dale looked at E. H. and asked, "Why?"

"I only know one way of telling you, so here goes; Dale, Pam has been in love with you for a while now. I imagine her feelings for you caused the look she gave you."

Dale laughed as he said, "E. H. that is ridiculous. She knows I care about her, but she's in love with me? I hardly think so." Dale said with an incredulous stare.

E. H. got up from the table and poured himself more coffee as he said, "Want more hot chocolate?"

Dale shook his head to indicate no, so E. H. continued, "Dale, I would never say such a thing unless I was sure. Love is a strange thing. If you doubt what I'm saying to you, ask someone else; ask Stanley."

"I don't think you would intentionally lie to me, E. H. What am I going to do if she is in love with me? I don't feel about her in that way. She is a friend, a perfect friend. I don't want to lead her on, but I can't tell her I'm not in love with her without hurting her. What can I say to her?"

"Dale, I've only been in love with one woman. Sara was that woman. Even though I knew she loved me as much as I loved her, I had to learn things. Women look at the world differently. It is neither bad nor good. It takes a lot of patience for two people in love to learn what makes the other happy. I doubt if I learned all the things about Sara." E. H. said.

Men are different from women, but I know if a woman feels dejected, she sometimes shows it by being angry or upset. You are going to have to figure out a way to let Pam know you love her like a sister and a friend." E. H. declared.

Suddenly, it sounded as if horses were coming down the hall. The kitchen door flew open, and Jordan and Skylar ran to E. H. They were both talking loudly when E. H. told them to use inside voices.

Skylar yelled, "The cowboy prince," and ran to hug him. Jordan straightened his stance, puffed his little chest out, and walked over for a handshake. Dale smiled and willed himself to put the Pam thing off for another day.

He enjoyed the innocence of the children and stayed until everyone was down for breakfast. When he was with the Denton's, he felt like he belonged to a family.

EPISODE 34

Rodney Medlin walked into his garage, where he saw Dale already working. He walked over to him and said, "Morning. You are at it early again. You have been here night and day for a few weeks. Are things OK with you?"

With an expressionless face, Dale said, "Just have a lot of thinking to do. Working helps me think."

"If you need some help, let me know. I can keep a secret if I need to." Rodney said.

"I appreciate it, but it is something I need to work out for myself," Dale answered.

Rodney tried again, "Woman problems?"

Dale was a bit irritated but controlled himself. "Just need time."

Rodney shook his head and walked over to the car he had been working on the day before. He was curious, but something about Dale made you believe you shouldn't mess around with him.

He reflected; *you have to watch out for the quiet ones; they will fight 'til the death if need be*. He turned and looked back at Dale and told himself, *and I'll find out what it is soon enough. Stonehope is too small to keep secretes.*

Dale went up to his apartment during lunch, heated a can of soup, and sat in front of the television watching the mid-day news. He didn't mean to doze off. When he heard someone knocking on the door, he stood in a daze and said, "Hold on, I'm coming."

Dale felt as if he was in a thick fog. He had been trying to warn Pam of the giant eightball rolling down a snowy street. He strumbled to the door and opened it. "Hey Stanley, I dozed off watching TV.

"Have you had lunch?" Dale asked

At first, Stanley thought Dale was drunk as he watched him stumble back to the couch. Stanley said, "I've already had lunch. I sensed I'd better come and see if you are alright. I haven't seen you in days."

What Stanley didn't say was Pam had sent him to check on Dale. It worried her he had not been to Edwards Diner in days. She thought maybe her being cool to him after the snow incident made him angry."

"I've been working hard for a few weeks," Dale said. He added, "I'm learning how to be a bachelor and trying my hand at cooking."

Stanley laughed and said, "How is it working out?"

A genuine smile lit up Dale's face, "I got the part about open can, pour in a pot, and turn heat low. I'm having a problem with toasting bread. The broiler on the stove is hard to regulate.

I guess I have blackened at least two loaves of bread. Rodney said beans were easy to cook, but he did not tell me they smelled terrible when you burn them; or that you had to throw the pot out." Dale said.

"Oh, that is what I smell. How about going with me to Edward's for dinner? They are having…."

Before Stanley could finish his sentence, Dale said, "No."

Stanley laughed again but stopped as suddenly as he started. Dale looked aggravated. Before he knew it, he said, "Pam is worried about you."

Dale rose from the couch and said, "I'm fine. I have to get back to work." He walked out the door and left Stanley sitting in the chair next to the couch.

Stanley stood up, walked out the door, and closed it behind him. He stood at the top of the stairs and saw Dale already at work on a car. He reasoned; *this is not like Dale. Now I'm worried.*

He walked down the stairs and left the garage. He headed to see E. H. Denton.

EPISODE 35

It was the first day of May, and Dwight Gacy woke with one focus. It was his birthday, and he is certain Pam will agree to go out with him. How could she resist?

He had purchased a new suit, shirt, tie, shoes, socks, and even underwear, black and silky. Dwight had heard the rumors for days about Pam and Dale breaking up. He aimed to repair her broken heart.

Once he made love to her, she would be his forever. After he showered, he sprayed expensive cologne over his body; it made him sneeze.

He walked into his bedroom and stood in front of the mirror, sucked in his belly, threw back his shoulders, and thought, *Pam, you are in for the best night of your life. Once you are in my arms, you will see Dale is just a boy; you need a man.*

What Dwight didn't know was Stanley arrived at Edwards Diner early and talked to Pam about what he learned from E. H. Denton.

He hated to tell Pam but thought it was better to know the truth. Stanley expected Pam to cry and to be upset. He did not expect Pam to smile, laugh, hug his neck and say he was a perfect friend.

Pam was upset but knowing the truth was better than what she imagined. She had felt unwanted and had been listless for days. She thought she did something to disgust Dale.

She felt she had been too forward. When she heard Dale thought of her as a little sister and a friend, it stung a bit, but she knew she had rather be that than not to know him at all.

She didn't want to get hopeful, but she had heard of friends growing closer, and eventually, they realized they were right for each other.

By the time Dwight arrived, she was flitting around the restaurant as if walking on air. Pam was thinking over and over; Dale doesn't hate me!

When she saw Dwight walk in, her shoulders drooped a bit. She hated to have to deal with the pig. She hated he didn't know what the word 'no' meant.

Dressed as if he were attending a funeral, Dwight walked over to his table; she said, "Who died?"

"You."

She felt chilled and felt sick to her stomach with his answer. He frightened her, but she asked, "What are you talking about?"

Dwight gave his sexiest smile. What Pam saw was a lecherous grin. He said, "You...long-legged, beautiful, sexy creature. Tonight, you will feel like you have died and gone to heaven. It will be my best birthday ever. He handed Pam a box wrapped with gold paper and ribbons and told her to open it.

Pam looked at the gift as if it was a bomb. She didn't know what to do. She didn't want it, but she was afraid to make him mad. Something about him always said you never wanted to make Dwight Gacy angry.

She said, "It is your birthday. Why are you giving me a present?" Pam put the gift on the table and walked away, saying, "I don't need a present from you?"

Anger flashed across Dwight's face. On his face was a wicked smile as he said loud enough for everyone in the restaurant to hear, "Don't be that way, Pam. We've known each other for a long time.

Let me take you out tonight, anywhere your heart desires. After we party, we'll get a room, and you will see what a real man is. I know you want me."

Pam threw up in her mouth. She continued to walk away. When she reached the counter, Dwight called out to the other patrons, "Today is my birthday, and Pam and I are going to party. I will make it a night for her to remember.

He tore the paper from the gift, opened it, and pulled out a bright red, strapless dress as he was talking. The dress was stunning, but when Pam saw it, the color drained from her face. She ran to the bathroom and threw up.

As Dwight was opening the gift, Dale walked in. He told Dwight he and Pam had already made plans for the evening. When Pam came back, she was relieved to see Dwight and the red dress were gone. The next thing she saw was Dale sitting at the bar hiding behind a menu.

She ran over and kissed him on the cheek. Dale was not expecting her reaction and said, "I have to tell you something."

Pam punched his arm and said, "Best friends forever. Don't stay away ever again. I have to punch my big brother once in a while to keep him in shape."

They both laughed, and Dale felt relieved. Later after Pam was off work, she found Dale in her driveway. He had been to Bo Jangles and bought take-out. She invited him inside.

They ate their chicken sandwiches, ate Oreo's, drank milk, and watched an old movie. When the movie was over, Dale stood up and said, "Pam, I have missed you. I'm sorry I acted so badly."

Pam pinched his cheek and said, "Dale, I could not ask for a better friend. And, thanks for saving me from Dwight. He gives me the creeps."

Dale's dream ran through his mind; Pam was ducking eight balls. But why did it come when she said Dwight Gacy's name like it was a dirty word.

He wanted to warn Pam, but he did not want to frighten her, so he just said, "Hey, make sure you check all your locks. I don't want anything to ever happen to you. You are the closest thing to a little sister I will ever have."

Pam smiled inside and outward as she and thought, *for now.* Three cars headed to Raleigh. The first car held E. H., Katherine, Jordan, and Skylar. In the second car were Martin and Dorothy Webb.

EPISODE 36

In the third car were Dale, Pam, and Stanley. They were going to the Fourth of July fireworks at the North Caroline State Fairgrounds. Everyone was excited.

The last two months had been uneventful, and time had flown. Dale was thinking about this as he drove along the bypass towards Raleigh. He was more familiar with the city since he and Pam sometimes rode around looking for different places to visit or eat.

Stanley often went with them on their Saturday outings since Dale convenience Pam Stanley was a good guy. Laughter was always around every corner, and the three friends enjoyed their friendships.

E. H. and Katherine were talking about how fast time had gone since the New Year Eve party at the church. The kids sat in the back. Jordan was playing a video game, and

Skylar talked to her imaginary friend, Star. Skylar would tell her mother Star wanted to know how much longer before the fireworks every few minutes.

They arrived at the fairground and parked where the state troopers told them to park. Once everyone was out of their vehicles, the group became a family. E. H. and his family enjoyed Dale and his friends.

Dale and his friends felt comfortable being around the Denton family. Dale enjoyed it more than he admitted. He never dreamed how much a real family would make him feel.

Sometimes Dale dredged up his reason for being in Blackstone County. In those times, he felt uncomfortable and gilt-ridden. He knew he would have to leave when the mission was over.

He treasured friendships, the feeling of belonging, and living like an average person. The mission end was coming up fast, and he hated to think of leaving the life he had found in the tiny town of Stonehope and the area of Blackstone County.

When it became dark, the fireworks began; the group of family and friends stood together watching. Dale was standing between Pam and Katherine.

He turned to Katherine and said, "I'm sorry Larry had to work. I wish he could be here."

"Me too," she said.

EPISODE 37

The demon dressed in black as he waited for his eyes to adjust to the dark. He sat cross-legged behind an azalea bush. It had only been fifteen minutes since his last cigar, but his craving for another was almost as intense as his craving for what he would do as soon as she came home.

He began planning the sequence in his mind. After she pulled up into the yard, he would wait until she got out. He knew she never varied from her routine, and this gave him a significant advantage.

By the time she opened her car door, he would pull his mask over his eyes, and he would be crouching behind the bush.

Her porch light was not repaired from his vandalism done nights before. She would have to get an electrician to fix it. When her car lights went out, he would ready himself. As she put the key into the front door lock, the door would open, and he would grab her from behind.

The man in black trembled with anticipation. Once he covered her nose and mouth with the chloroformed cloth, he would drag her inside. When in the house, he would wait until she woke up; the real fun would begin.

Pam yelled, "Cooksey, I've done everything out here. I'm going home. See you in the morning."

"I'm almost finished too. See you at five," Cooksey said as he peeked through the window which was between the kitchen and dining area and added, "Don't be late."

As usual, Pam smiled. Cooksey always told her not to be late, and usually, she was the one opening the door in the morning. He was always fifteen minutes late.

Pam would be the one to turn everything on and do the setup. He would look sheepish as he walked in and apologized as he put the change into the cash register. It was always the same.

Pam rubbed her lower spine as she walked out the door and thought it was *time to get some new shoes*. Her car was under the outside area light, but she looked around before she continued.

She was always afraid someone would think she had the restaurant cash. Whenever she mentioned her fear, Cooksey would always say the same thing, "Everyone knows we go to the bank each afternoon at four-thirty. No one in this town will bother either one of us for the small amount of change we have on hand.

Besides, the deputies take turns coming to check on us and usually drive into the parking lot about the time we close up."

Pam knew Cooksey was right, but she had not seen a deputy come in or drive around this night. When Pam reached her car, she bent down to look underneath. Suddenly a car turned into the gravel parking lot of the store. Pam turned around. She immediately began to tremble and to breathing heavily.

Her eyes were wide as she saw the deputy get out of his cruiser, "What the heck, Jackson. You scared me to death. Deputies are supposed to make us feel safe, not terrified."

"Damn, Pam, you are looking good tonight. Your eyes are glowing. Want to go have a little fun?" Devin Jackson said.

Pam wanted to walk over and slap his youthful face, but she said, "Thought your curfew was at eight, Jackson. I didn't know they let kids drive cruisers after eight. You better get along home to your mama before you get into trouble."

Jackson countered a taunt of his own, "Miss Pam, you can change my diaper any time. Jackie Boy needs a little cuddling tonight, and I want you to tuck me in. He finished with a big laugh and blew Pam a kiss.

"Not tonight, Jackie Boy; I'm too tired."

Before Pam got into her car, she checked the back seat. All was clear, so she opened the door, sat in the seat, and looked in her rear-view mirror as she locked all the doors.

Her hair stood up on her arms, and she felt chilled. She shook her head and wondered, *Pam, why are you so jumpy tonight*.

She started the car and remembered what had been happening in the small towns in the area. She turned her cd player loud enough to drown out her thoughts and began to sing to the first song she and Dale had line danced to; 'These Arms' by Dwight Yoakam. Even though she was smiling at the memories of Dale's first line dance, Pam couldn't shake the feeling of apprehension. She turned the music louder and began singing as loud as she could.

Fifteen minutes later, she turned into her driveway; she was still singing as she turned her car off and looked at the broken porch light. She wished it were working and thought, tomorrow I will call the electrician Stanley mentioned to me.

She also wished she had a more up-to-date car so the lights would automatically stay on when she got out. *Maybe one day*, she said to herself.

When Pam got out of the car, she smelled something familiar, but she couldn't put her finger on it. She walked onto the porch, put the key into the door lock, and opened the door.

Suddenly the smell was powerful, and someone was holding something on her face; another scent. Her senses and her body were shutting down as someone strong held her tightly around her waist.

Dale lay on the couch. The TV was on as he slept through the eleven o'clock news. Suddenly Dale sat up, looking wildly around the room. "What the" He smelled something and ordered his brain to figure it out. Thinking out loud, he said, "It's a cigar."

He stood up and scanned the one-room apartment for the culprit. He saw no one. He opened the bathroom door quickly expected to see someone; no one was there. He walked around the room, checking the window and door locks; all were secure.

Dale turned off the TV and walked around the room sniffing. The smell was gone, but he knew who smoked that kind of cigar. He felt like the smell was a foreshadowing of something which would happen soon, an omen of evil.

He went to the refrigerator, took the milk carton out, and drank from it as he wondered, *did I have a terrible dream or is someone I know in trouble? I'm usually more in tune with my senses. Does someone need me? I don't know what to do.*

Dale paced from one side of the room to the other. His five senses heightened, but his sixth sense was failing him. He grabbed his car keys and rushed out of the room. He drove by Stanley's house. His car was there, and the place was dark; nothing looked amiss.

He decided to drive by Pam's house before he drove out to the Denton's. He moved slowly down the street. When he reached her house, he stopped and put a window down.

Her car was there, and the porch light was off. The curtains closed, and a faint light showed through. He knew Pam had several night lights, so nothing looked amiss. As he drove off, he heard something. He stopped. A black cat ran across Pam's small yard with a yapping dog close behind. He smiled and put his window up but as he drove away but the feeling lingered.

When he drove by the Denton family home, all was dark.

EPISODE 38

When Pam opened her eyes, she was staring at the ceiling in her bedroom. She assumed she had fallen asleep with her uniform on and had a terrible nightmare. She tried to turn over and curl into the fetal position.

Suddenly, she realized someone was standing beside her bed. She reached for the nightstand drawer to get her pistol. The person slammed the drawer, catching and crushing two of Pam's fingers.

She tried to scream as a purple gloved hand covered her mouth. The man again put the cloth over her nose and mouth, and she quickly blacked out.

When Pam woke this time, she realized her hands and feet were spread-eagle and tied to her bed. Sweet-smelling cigar smoke permeated the room. The terror in her mind raced throughout her body like an electric current.

She looked from side to side several times, trying to grasp what was happening to her. Then she raised her head and looked between her breasts. The room was dark except for the night light on the opposite wall.

She opened her mouth to scream just as a pair of her dirty socks forced into her mouth. She began breathing through her nose rapidly. She tried to push the socks out with her tongue, but they didn't move.

He was putting tape over her mouth and the socks. She raised her head and looked again. She saw a man in surgical gloves, a mask over his head and face. She tried to talk, but only guttural sounds came.

She bit down on the socks and whipped her head back and forth until she willed herself to stop. Pam's head rose again to see her jailer smoking a small cigar through the mouth of a Freddy Krueger mask.

Pam wondered how long she was out. The room was a cloud of smoke. She realized her nose was burning, and her eyes were watering. The terror once again went through her body as it became stiff with fear. In her fear, she could not remember where she had smelled the sweet, odorous smoke.

He got up and walked to the side of the bed. Pam watched him as he took off the mask. She knew him! She looked frantically around the room, searching for a way out of her predicament. The person looked at her with a sickening smile, a smile she knew well.

"Hello, Sweet pea," he said as he pulled a long hunting knife from its sheath. "Before I get started, I want to tell you I am the one who killed your son. He was a little piece of shit and a rat."

Pam's anger made her feel as if she could come out of the restraints and choke him, but she couldn't do it. She softly cried as she watched him.

He ran his finger along the blade, cutting through the glove and cutting his finger. Without taking his eyes from Pam, he pulled his glove off, put his finger in his mouth, and sucked the blood.

She studied his face as his eyebrows raised, and he smiled. It was as if he was playing with a child. He put the cut glove into his right front pants pocket and pulled out another one from his back pocket.

After he put on the new glove, he popped it against his wrist. The pleasure in his face made Pam shut her eyes. She silently prayed, Please, God, don't let him hurt me.

With her eyes still closed, she felt the tip of the knife blade rest on her cheek under her right eye. She dared not move and kept her eyes closed as the blade move from her face to her uniform. He cut each button from her uniform top, and then he gently slipped the knife under the middle of her bra.

When she felt the terror could get no worse, she felt him cut and then pull away her bra cups. Ashes fell on her right breast and burned her skin.

He said, "Open your eyes, Pam."

Oh, my god, what are you going to do to me, Pam thought. The horrid question came as she closed her eyes again and realized she knows him!

She opened her eyes and looked frantically around the room. She wanted to ask why he was doing this.

When she saw his revolting, disgusting smile, it sickened her.

The news of the last few months went through her mind. Although she couldn't speak, her brain said, this is the killer of seven women. Pictures were flashing through her brain as she remembered hearing details of his madness. She knew what he was going to do to her.

He could see the same repulsed face Pam had when she did not want his gift. He slapped her. "Open your eyes, girl!"

When she opened her eyes, he gave her a lecherous look she had seen many times before. He always made her feel like she should take a shower each time he left the restaurant.

He taunted her, saying, "I should have taken you somewhere else, girl. I want to take those socks out and kiss your full lips."

He threw his head back and laughed, saying, "Then I would find another use for your sweet pink mouth. It's a shame I can't, but I'll find some other ways of thrilling you. I've been wantin' you for a long time."

He became quiet as he slowly cut her clothes, pulled them from underneath her, and dropped them on the floor. Every time Pam closed her eyes, he would hit her, sometimes with his fist. She finally chose to leave them open and look at the ceiling.

When he had cut all her clothes away, he sat on the bed and began rubbing the knife's blade all over Pam's body. Then he put on a condom, mounted her, and raped her.

No matter how hard she prayed for it, she did not pass out. She tried to think of things that made her happy. She wanted to live, and she hoped if she didn't fight, he would not kill her.

But she knew it was a lie. She had seen him, and he wasn't about to let her live; this man brutally killed all the others.

She raised her head and looked right into her face. He could smell the fear, and it excited him. He got up, lit another cigar, and sat down beside her again. This time he used the hunting knife to make cuts. Trickles of blood began to snake down her body as Pam's tears silently ran down both sides of her face.

She began silently saying the 23rd Psalm over and over. By the time he mounted her again, she was in another place, and instead of seeing his scruffy, disgusting face, she saw the face of her son, Teddy.

Mercifully, she passed out. After the last cut, he thrust the knife between her ribs and into her heart. He removed the knife from her chest and flipped her over. He drew a giant happy face on her back. He then removed the condom and put it in his right front pants pocket.

Time had gone by faster than he realized, and he thought, *I've been enjoying this one too much. I can't risk taking her outside to my truck.*

He rubbed his hand between her legs and smiled. He reached down and picked up her shredded panties and put them in the same pocket with the two purple surgical gloves and the condom.

He pulled the bedsheet from underneath Pam and looked around to see if he left anything. He balled the sheet up, gathered her clothes, and put it under his arm. He slithered out the back door and away to his truck, located two blocks over.

EPISODE 39

When Cooksey drove up to Edward's Diner, he was fifteen minutes late. He noticed the lights were off in the restaurant. He looked around for Pam's car.

"What the," she is never late."

Cooksy parked and went inside. He began turning on the lights and hurried to the kitchen because he would open the doors in fifteen more minutes. He rushed around to turn everything on, made the coffee, made the biscuits, and put them in the oven.

He began frying the ham and sausage. At which point, it was time to open the front door. He thought *Pam has never been late. This is not like her.*

Cooksey checked on the ham and sausage and then removed the change bag from the small safe. As he was putting the money in the cash register, Stanley walked in.

"Cooksey, your face is red. What is going on?"

"Pam is not here, and I am behind. Let me give you a cup of coffee while I take up the meat." Cooksey said.

Stanley sat quietly at the bar with his coffee, waiting for Pam to come in so he could order. After Cooksey took all the meat from the grill, the biscuits from the oven, and returned to the counter. Stanley asked, "Have you called Pam?"

"Haven't had time; will you call her?" he asked.

Stanley dialed Pam's land line. It rang several times. He tried calling her cell phone, and when there was no answer, he furrowed his brows and yelled out to Cooksey in the kitchen. "Hey Cooksey, I do not get an answer on her cell phone or her house phone."

As Stanley yelled, Johnny Edwards walked into his restaurant for another day's work. "What is going on?" he asked Stanley.

Stanley turned to Johnny and said, "Pam is late, and Cooksey is trying to do both jobs."

Johnny said, "Pam has never been late. Has anyone tried to call her?"

"Yes, I tried her cell and house phone. No answer," Stanley answered.

During their exchange, four customers had walked in and sat down. They were waiting for someone to take their order.

Johnny walked over so he could speak to the men saying, "Our waitress is not here yet. Please give me a couple of minutes, and I will take your order.

Johnny Edwards then headed for the kitchen to see what was happening. When he came out, he went over to each of the two tables and took their order.

Each minute that passed seemed to be longer than the next as Stanley sat wondering about Pam. He wrote his cell phone number on a napkin and yelled to the two men in the kitchen, "I'm going over to Pam's house and check on her."

Johnny walked out as Stanley added, "My phone number is on this napkin. Call me if she shows up."

"Yeah, man. Call me when you find Pam." Johnny Edwards said.

EPISODE 40

Dale began working before daylight. As he descended the apartment stairs, he heard his boss, Rodney, working inside the art garage. He also saw Junior Maddox drive up on his Jaguar, get out, and bang on the art room door.

Junior overlooked Dale as he yelled, "Damn it, Rodney, I know you are in there. Open the goddam door."

Dale watched as his boss, Rodney Medlin, open the door for Junior. Immediately he heard the two men yelling. He kept working until Junior came out, went to his car, and left squalling tires.

When Rodney came out, there was no doubt about his anger. Dale could see Rodney's lips pressed tightly together, his face red, and his fist clenched.

As he walked towards the back of the mechanic shop, he hit his foot on a bucket of bolts. Rodney picked up the bucket and tossed it across the floor as if it were a bucket of Styrofoam peanuts. He then began to use every curse word he knew.

Dale kept working on the engine of the ford truck. He wanted to ask Rodney if he were okay, but he did not. *Not a good time*, he thought.

Dale's phone rang, "Hey, Stanley."

Before Dale could say anything else, Stanley asked, "Have you heard from Pam?"

"No. Why?"

"She did not show up for work this morning."

"Maybe she didn't feel well," Dale answered.

Stanley said, "I've tried her on both phones, and Cooksey said she had never missed a day."

"Have you been to her house?"

"I'm headed there now."

"I'll leave here and meet you there," Dale said as he worried about the uneasy feelings he continued to have.

Stanley was already at Pam's house when Dale arrived. He saw Pam's car was there.

As soon as Dale opened his car door, Stanley started talking. "I-I knocked on the d-d-door and been to every w-w-window and c-c-called her n-n-name. She's not a-a-answering."

Dale could see Stanley had a creased forehead, his eyes were large, and he was rubbing his hand in his hair. He walked over and put his hand on Stanley's shoulder. "Calm down, man."

Stanley started to speak again when Devin Jackson drove up in his patrol car. He got out and walked towards the two men. "What's going on, Stanley. You sounded panicked."

Before Stanley could start stuttering again, Dale said, "Pam did not show up for work. Stanley has called her cell and her land line. He has knocked on the door and walked around outside the house calling her, but she has not responded."

"She was fine when I saw her last night. Do either one of you have a key?" said Devin.

Stanley looked at Dale. "No, I do not have a key," answered Dale.

The three walked up onto the stoop and took turns calling Pam's name. Suddenly Devin's elbow shot out, and the window in the front door broke.

"Damn, I stumbled," said Devin.

Both Dale and Stanley looked at Devin, understanding what he did on purpose. Devin reached inside, turned the dead-bolt, and then the door lock; the door opened.

Devin said, "Stay out here. I will look around."

Again, Dale and Stanley looked at each other, but they stood waiting for Devin to look around Pam's home.

When Devin came back out the door, Stanley thought he looked like a ghost. He asked, "Is she in there?"

Before answering, Devin closed the door and stood. He pulled out his radio and called the sheriff's office to send Detective Cain and Detective Perez.

Dale tried to push Devin away from the door as he said, "Let me go in."

Devin stood firm and said, "No man, you do not want to go in there."

Without a second thought, Dale put his hand on each side of Officer Jackson's arms, picked him up as if he were a doll, set him out of his way, and went inside.

Within seconds Dale came out the door, went down the steps, bent over, and vomited on the lawn. Stanley was still frozen and could not speak.

The detectives drove up as Dale told Stanley Pam was dead and not to go in the house.

EPISODE 41

The temperature was in the low-eighties, the air was still, and the humidity insufferable. Distant thunder rumbled in the distance as Pam Mann's graveside funeral services began. Her closest friends sat in one row of funeral home chairs beside the casket, waiting for the minister to speak.

Dale, Stanley, Larry, Katherine, E. H., and the Martins sat in the first row under the funeral tent. They were Pam's family. No one knew if she had a family. They did not know from where Pam came. She had just shown up years earlier with her fourteen-year-old son.

What no one at the funeral knew was how hard life had been for Pam. She had run away from a drug-related and abusive relationship. She planned for her and Teddy never to go back or found.

When she first arrived, Pam rented a cheap room from an older woman in Stonehope. She enrolled her son, Teddy, in the local school and took the waitress job at Edwards Diner.

During her son's senior year of high school, he began talking to his mother about not fitting in. She had told him to hang in and plan to go into the military after he graduated. She did not know that the boys Teddy called his friends were pressuring him to do drugs, which was one reason they had moved.

When his good grades plummeted, Teddy went to the councilor's office. Teddy told the counselor about the boys who were bullying him into taking drugs. He also told her he was going into the Marines after graduation, but before leaving, he would go to the sheriff and tell him about the students selling drugs.

Teddy did not know his soft-spoken, pretty counselor was the one selling the drugs to his classmate. Two days later, someone found Teddy in Stonehope's graveyard, dead because of a forced overdose.

Pam never told anyone, not even Dale. However, Stanley and others had heard the rumors.

The minister of E. H. Denton's church had met her a few times during gatherings at the church. While her friends looked at the flower-covered casket, the minister read a few Bible verses and spoke of how much Pam's friends cared for her. He mentioned her smiling face every day as she took care of the patrons who visited Edwards Diner.

When finished, he nodded to Dale, crying silently as tears rolled down his cheeks. Dale stood up, walked to the casket, and added another rose to the casket spray.

The roses on the casket spray were sprayed with fake snow—also, snowballs and Baby's the spray. Only Dale, E. H., and Stanley knew the meaning of the snow and snowballs.

When Dale sat back down, the minister nodded toward the funeral director, and the casket lowered into the ground.

The minister walked over and whispered to each of the people sitting in the chairs. As he did, the other people who had come began to mingle and spoke to Dale and his friends.

Most of the attendees had been patrons of Edwards Restaurant. However, Sheriff Maddox, Detective Cain, Detective Perez, and a few other deputies were also there.

Dale noticed a lady about Pam's age. He walked over and introduced himself. The woman said, "I've heard a lot of things about you. Pam thought you were the one."

"I don't understand," replied Dale.

"My name is Sea. I have been friends with Pam since we were in grade school. I'm going to miss her."

"Sea. Yes, she mentioned you. I'm glad she had a friend to visit. It seemed to me she worked all the time."

Sea said, "Good to meet you. I see why she loved you, and I am happy she had time with you."

As the tears ran down his cheek, Dale said, "That's for letting me know. I'm going to miss my dear friend."

Sea hugged Dale gently and walked away.

Stanley, E. H., and Dale were the last ones to leave. The thunder was louder, and the wind began blowing as Dale looked back towards the grave before climbing into E. H.'s truck. He supposed; *I know she must be happy beside her son*. His next thought was, *now I will catch the son-of-a-bitch who killed her if it is the last thing I ever do.*

EPISODE 42

Once again, Sheriff Maddox arrived home to an empty house, went into his bedroom, and changed clothes. Pam Mann's funeral had gotten to him. He remembered when her son died and how upset she had been.

He also remembered he had not pressed on the investigation of Teddy Mann's death. He had known about the drug trafficking at the school and who ultimately was behind it.

Since then, he had eaten many times at the diner, and Pam had always been polite and respectful. Today during the service, he thought about her kindness and how he had let her down. His thoughts were perplexing as he felt his whole being had changed.

Vernon Maddox felt like he was a different man, and he knew why. He missed Pearl more and more every day. He knew she would be disappointed and sickened about how he had run the Blackstone Sheriff's Department in the past.

He had to change it because he wanted to be a man she could love and trust with their daughter; he wanted them to be a family.

After he dressed in his regular clothes, he went into the kitchen, opened the refrigerator, and grabbed himself a drink; a Mt. Dew.

He sat at the table and took out his cell phone, and called Detective Perez.

EPISODE 43

E. H. pulled the truck into the driveway of his longtime family home, parked in his usual spot, turned the engine off, and sat staring at nothing. All of a sudden, someone hit the side of the truck.

E. H. jumped, and his right hand quickly moved to his chest. He looked out the window and saw Martin standing and laughing so hard he could hardly catch his breath.

Uncharacteristically, E. H. sternly said, "What the devil, Martin."

The laughter stopped, and the smile was gone. Martin said, "Sorry, E. H."

E. H. smiled as he opened the truck door. He stepped out of his truck, closed the door, turned to Martin, and said, "I just took the kids to school. They were full of energy today. Somedays, it's a lot to handle."

Martin didn't reply. He knew what E. H. was saying. He and Dorothy raised one son all the years, and now they were helping raise Stephen's children when they could.

They sent money to Atlanta, where Stephen's wife, Anna, lived, but they rarely saw them. Martin and Dorothy had wanted other children, but Martha never became pregnant again after the horrible event.

The two men walked to the porch and went in the back door. Martin pulled the chair back from the table and sat down while E. H. made a pot of coffee. Martin was looking down at his hands, thinking about how much he still missed Stephen.

E. H. went to the bathroom and came back into the kitchen. He took two coffee mugs from the cabinet and waited.

He remembered a time before Martin married his sister, Dorothy. Martin had always been a good and godly man. He also knew he had been carrying a heavy load since his son, Stephen, was killed in action.

He filled the cups with coffee and sat down at the table with his brother-in-law and friend, and said, "Hey, Martin, how long have we been friends?"

Since we were both in diapers, I guess; too many years to talk about," said Martin.

As the two men sat, Martin began to talk about their most famous and dangerous adventure.

The two had been friends since they were children and had lived less than a mile apart. Martin's family-owned and ran Webb's Mill and E. H.'s family farmed.

The men had worked in their family's trade since they were young boys. However, they both still found time to get into trouble.

The one they reminisced most was the water over the damn incident. It was funny to E. H. and Martin but not their parents. The boys were almost nine when they decided to walk over the Webb's Mill dam beside the running mill.

The diverted water ran the grinding gears of the old mill from the Tar River into something that resembled a concrete box culvert but had no top.

You could stand on the side and watch the huge gears tuning because of the flow of water. The water ran in and out and made the gears turn; the ones inside the mill made the grinding stone turn and produced Webb's Mill Cornmeal, a local favorite.

On a hot July day, the boys were on the bank of the Tar River, near the bottom of the Webb's Mill dam. They were trying to throw rocks across the rushing water of the river.

They tried for over an hour, throwing one small stone after the other. Soon E. H. and Martin became bored, and they sat down trying to think of something else to occupy their time.

The other side of the river had a sand bank and a swirling pool only about a foot deep. Martin said, "Sure would be nice to be swimming."

"Sure, but we will have to walk up the road to the bridge and walk over the bridge. You know our pa's said to stay off the bridge," said E. H.

Martin had grinned and punched E. H. in the arm and said, "I know a way, and we won't have to walk over the bridge."

"What we gonna do? Fly?" laughed E. H.

"Follow me," Martin said as he started climbing back up the bank towards the mill. He looked around and did not see anyone, so he climbed up the rocks beside the concrete encasement which held the mill gears. He turned and looked at E. H. and said, "Come on!"

"Are you crazy, Martin? Don't climb on the encasement. If you fall into those gears, it will be like that sausage grinder your mama uses!" yelled E. H.

Martin made a sound like a chicken clucking and threw his head back and laughed. He began climbing up the rocks towards the ten-inch-thick concrete encasement wall and looked back at E. H. He hollered over the sound of the turning gears, "You comin'?"

E. H. was scared, but he followed Martin, and they walked the perimeter until they reached the dam. It was easy since the diverted water flowed into the gear's encasement instead of going across the dam.

Without looking back at his best friend, Martin stepped onto the dry eighteen-inch wide damn. He held his arms out for balance and continued across the Webb's Mill dam.

When he reached the other side, he jumped off the dam onto a concrete pad. He turned to see E. H. only a couple of feet behind him. When E. H. jumped onto the pad, Martin started jumping up and down and clapping, "We did it!"

The color came back into E. H.'s face as he joined in the celebration. "Yeah, weren't nothin' to it."

The two boys left the concrete pad and made their way towards the sand bar. With their clothes still on they jumped into the whirlpool twirling in the sandy cove. They began splashing each other.

Eventually, they climbed up on the sandy shore and made little sailboats with pieces of driftwood and large leaves. The boys watched them go around and around in the whirlpool.

They gathered small rocks and threw at the sailboats pretending they were pirate ships. After they sank all their sail boats, they lay back on the sand looking at the clouds. "That one looks like an elephant," said E. H.

"That one looks like our arithmetic teacher," said Martin. Both boys started laughing and rolling in the sand.

E. H. asked, "What time is it? I'm hungry."

"Me too," said Martin and added "let's go to my house. Mama had biscuits left from lunch. We can put some jelly on them."

Both boys jumped up and looked at each other. E. H. said, "We crossing on the bridge or the dam?"

"It's shorter on the dam. You go first this time. I'll be right behind you," replied Martin.

With no idea it was near the five o'clock shut down time for the mill grinding stone E. H. and Martin started across the dam.

To the tune of the song 'She'll Be Coming 'Round the Mountain' the boys were loudly singing, "We'll be coming over the dam when we come."

Neither saw or heard Martin's father waving his arms and yelling. When they were about three feet from the other side and near the encasement wall, Webb's Mill shut down the grinding wheels and closed the encasement.

The water began to run over the dam instead of through the encasement. Quickly the water went from an inch to three inches deep and kept rising.

Both boys froze. E. H. peed on himself as Martin screamed, "Jump." E. H. took one long step and jumped toward the encasement wall. He landed on the wall with his belly, and Martin jumped and landed on top of him.

Martin was holding onto E. H. as the water increased to its usual ten-inch-deep flow over the dam. E. H. couldn't move as the water tugged at his feet, and he began to yell for help.

Just as the boys thought they were going to die, someone pulled Martin from E. H.'s back. E. H. tried to raise his feet from the fast-flowing water. It caused him to tip on the encasement wall towards the gears.

In a flash, he realized the gears were not turning, so he raised his legs upward to fall into the encasement instead of being dragged by the water running over the dam.

Just as E. H. tipped forward, he felt someone grab the back of his shirt and lift him from the encasement. He hung limp like a dead fish as Martin's father carried him down the rocks beside the encasement where Martin was already standing.

They knew they both were going to get a whipping, and they did. E. H. and Martin were also banned from Webb's Mill unless they were with their parents.

It was now just a funny memory the men would sometimes tell others. They had many stories which became enhanced over the years, but the dam story was the funniest and the scariest time of their young lives.

Martin and E. H. sat a few minutes quietly, cherishing the memories. Martin spoke first, "Need to go check on Dorothy and see if she needs help with anything." He stood and said, "This was good, E. H. Thanks."

E. H. looked up at Martin and said, "Yeah."

EPISODE 44

Dale sat at the work bench, reading a new manual on audio systems. Stanley was having problems with his, and he had asked Dale to help. Stanley's main concern was someone hacked his car's Wi-Fi system.

Neither of them had spoken out loud about their concerns, but both knew what could happen if it had. They had become close over the months and sometimes seemed to mirror each other's thoughts without speaking.

Dale heard Rodney come out of the art room. He turned around and started laughing. Rodney was holding a yellow and green metal flower in each hand.

"That's a new way to use gears, Rodney," Dale said and then asked, "Who is the lucky lady?"

Rodney smiled and said, "Dorothy Webb. Martin came in and said she saw some on Pinterest and told him it was what she wanted for Christmas. She printed out a picture, and he brought it to me along with farm equipment parts. What do you think?"

"Looks like you have a new career and a green thumb," Dale chuckled.

"Yeah, it is different from my other metal sculptors, but I will add them to my catalog," Rodney answered.

Dale said, "Catalog?

Rodney said, "I had someone to make a web page for me, and I have an online catalog."

"How is it going?" asked Dale.

Rodney walked over and laid the flowers on the counter and said, "It just went online last Saturday, but I already have five orders for sculptors."

Surprised, Dale said, "It's a good idea, and I wish you luck." But he couldn't help but remember the other things Rodney was doing in his art room.

Rodney looked at the flower with a strange expression before he said, "Maybe we will enlarge the art shop, and you can help me keep up with my orders."

"Sure thing," Dale said, knowing he would be leaving his job and Blackstone County in a few more months.

EPISODE 45

Dale Weaver turned into Stanley's driveway and parked his truck. He sat there a couple of minutes, waiting for Stanley. When Stanley came out of the door, he had a tense look on his face.

He walked to the passenger side of the truck, opened the door, and got in. He looked at Dale and gave him a big smile. Dale was relieved.

Summoned to a home outside of Wake Forest, Dale and Stanley began guessing what kind of meeting it would be. The only thing they knew about the meeting was Inrun52 had called, and it was slated as a Banana alert, meaning it was a yellow alert, and the next and final alert would be the red Apple.

Neither man had been involved in these undercover alerts before. They were virgins when it came to an actual take-down.

Before Dale backed out of the driveway, Stanley asked, "Are we ears?"

"No," Dale answered and added, "The Wi-Fi is off, and I swept the truck for other electronic devices. We are driving blind and deaf. I also unhooked the radio, so no music."

Stanley asked, "Are you nervous?"

"I guess we both feel about the same. If we make an error, we are dead, and probably others will be too. It's sobering."

"Yep," Stanley's replied.

Stanley was the one with the directions to the meeting house. After leaving 64 Highway, there were only two turns.

They were in a rural area where they passed old homes, farming acreage, and occasional newer homes of successful farmers and people who worked in Raleigh or surrounding areas.

When Dale made the last turn, he saw several huge homes which probably sold for millions of dollars. Stanley then had him turn within the community two times and finally pointed to the driveway.

Stanley noted, "There is a three-car garage. I wonder if we are the only ones here."

"I don't know. Let's go in and see."

Before they were up the numerous steps, the front door opened. Inrun52 was smiling and said, "Hurry in. You are the last ones here."

Dale and Stanley looked at each other and then followed Inrun52 through the house, down several steps into a large basement. There was a large table where five other people sat. Both men had the same involuntary reflex. Their mouths opened when they saw people they knew.

Dale whispered what the... and Stanley verbalized the same response as the other participants had similar reactions.

Inrun52 said, "Sit down, agents."

After Stanley sat, he held the stare of Sunny Tupelo. Both were astonished. As close as they were, they had no idea the other would be there.

While Stanley's focus was on one person, Dale looked around to see Rodney Medlin, the garage owner, and Martin Webb, the brother-in-law of E. H. He then glanced around to see Cooksey, the restaurant, and Rooster seen cooking barbecue at the church. Dale was filled with multiple questions and did not hear Stanley stuttering.

Inrun52 stood up and loudly uttered three words "Hold your questions."

Everyone around the table looked up at their handler standing before them. She then began talking. "All of you have some knowledge about everyone at this table. You all play a part in the drug ring's takedown, which plagues a large amount of North Carolina.

You are some of the best and most trusted agents involved in this takedown. There are others who you will never know. Knowing them would not enhance your part."

Everyone relaxed a little while listening to their handler. Inrun52 continued, "The seven of you will be dependent on each other. If anyone does not do their job, the take down may not happen. It may mean the death of all of you. I have vetted every one of you and worked with most of you for years.

I trust all of you, and I am telling you to trust each other. However, if you see someone failing to do their part or they are putting you in danger, you must eliminate that person."

The people around the table looked at each other. The seriousness of the situations was sinking deep within them. They all had their life on the line for the mission.

They were all gears in a machine, and if one broke, the others would follow. On the other hand, they all trusted Inrun52 unequivocally, so therefore, they trusted each other.

Inrun52 was watching each facial expression and the body language of each person at the table. When she was satisfied each had understood the gravity of their situation, she said, "We will take a little break and have refreshments. As you see, food and drinks are on the counter. Help yourself. You will have ten minutes, and you may talk to your fellow agents."

Once their break was over, Inrun52 put them through several physical trust exercises. Even though these exercises were a critical part of their trust-building, you might expect laughter and silliness with small kids. As they went through the activities, Inrun52 could see them relax and relate to each other positively.

At this point, Cooksey helped her set up the ingredients for sandwiches and more liquid options to wash down the food. There was much more talking than at the first break. Inrun52 spoke during the lunch period; however, she spent a lot more mental energy observing the bonds between people in the group.

After the forty-minute lunch break, everyone cleared their food and drinks from the table and sat waiting for Inrun52 to begin. Her first words were, "I believe in each one of you and you as a group. The significance of today will halt the cogs of this drug machine for a time."

"We all know there will be replacements as soon as we bring down this organization, but as I have mentioned to all of you, this take down will allow us to get more undercover agents in place for the next campaign. We may not win the war yet, but we will keep winning battles."

Inrun52 walked away from the table and retrieved her oversized purse. She reached inside and pulled out a stack of documents.

Each document contained several pieces of paper stapled together, and all seven agents received a set. When the passing of documents was over, she identified the documents as plans for a first-run event.

"As you know, the street-name for the leader of this cartel is Brutus. On March 15, he is giving a party at the Stonehouse Farm to celebrate the Ides of March. This event is an exercise, a practice of sorts. Dale and Stanley will valet and keep an eye on the people who are coming in.

Martin, Cooksey, and Rooster will be in charge of the food. Rodney will be acting as one of the bartenders, and Sunny will be attending as a guest. Each person will do their job normally but keep your eyes open for any actions which may seem unusual."

"You will see a map of the property on one of the pages I passed around. Also, there is a layout of the house. You will notice on the map there are two buildings colored red. These buildings are where the drugs are stored and where they wait for transport to several areas east of Raleigh."

"Above ground, these two buildings look alike and are old tobacco barns; however, they have concrete basements under each. The drug storage areas cannot be reached from inside the tobacco barns."

"The red tobacco barn marked A is reached by a tunnel which begins in the tack room. The red barn marked B is reached by a tunnel over two-hundred-fifty feet long.

The entry of this tunnel is in the library of the main house. There is a secret door that looks like part of a bookshelf. Who would care to guess the name of the book which activates the secrete door?"

Sunny Tupelo spoke up, "I assume it is a book about Julius Caesar."

"You are right," said Inrun52, and she continued. "There is a tunnel between barn A and barn B, divided by a steel door with an iris scanner, and that is the only way the door will open. Both sides of the door have to be activated."

"Brutus' eye scan from the library tunnel opens his side, and from the tack room, the eye scan of the soft-spoken and unassuming stable cleaner named Cotton opens the door.

Some of you already knew him and had no idea he is such a valuable cog in the drug organization wheel. His help will be invaluable."

"Look at the aerial picture in your folders. See the large building with the blue metal roof?" said Inrun52. Everyone nodded to indicate they did, and she continued. "This building houses 12 high-priced horses and the tack room I just mentioned. When you look at the building from the back, it appears to be only the rear of the stable with a large concrete pad."

"If you look closely, you will notice tire marks from vehicles which have driven up to the wall by using this concrete pad and later backed out. The tracks seem to have disappeared into the wall.

Yes, the trucks disappear, but only because there is an oversized garage behind the horse areas. The doors to this garage opened by someone inside. This person operates double doors, which allow the vehicles to go into the private garage."

"On the day of the raid, Cotton will be that person. He must stay in character in case Junior or any of his minions see him talking with you. If another person is there, you must treat Cotton as an enemy but don't harm him, and if you must, try not to make it a fatal wound."

"The vehicles inside are housed to transport drugs and money. There are two RVs that families use for camping to destinations order by Brutus.

These families get a great vacation and receive a large amount of cash for doing so. There are also brand-named delivery trucks and some not so new automobiles and trucks with hidden compartments."

When Inru52 mentions the hidden compartments, Dale glanced at Rodney and felt a sense of relief before quickly returning his attention to Inrun52.

"To illustrate the scope of Brutus, I will remind you of the 18-wheeler authorities stopped on I-95 a couple of years ago. The truck with cases of groceries and three boxes of cash; four and a half million in cash."

"Why didn't we catch him then? We needed more information about the bottom rungs of Brutus' ladder. As I said before, we will halt the cogs of this drug machine for a time and send in more long-term agents so we can stay in the fight."

Inrun52 noticed some attendees appeared to be tiring, so she said, "We're done for today. I thank you for coming and for your attention, but there is one more thing I need to stress. The Ides of March party is not the takedown, so be careful not to expose what you know."

"Dale, you are the only one who has not been on The Stonehouse compound. The rest of you have been on this compound for several events. Take your cues from them. The real take-down will be soon enough. The July 4th event at The Stonehouse will be like none before."

"I will not talk to you again before the main event in July. Again, keep your eyes open at the March event, and if you see suspicious activities, stay levelheaded and know all your experience will help us succeed in July. Now, please pass all paperwork to me. It will be shredded and destroyed."

After a pause, Inrun52 asked, "Are there any questions we need to address?"

Martin Webb stood and said, "This is not a question, but we want Dale to know we are glad to have him aboard."

"I have a question said Stanley, and he proceeded, "Can you tell us what part Sunny will play in the takedown?"

Inrun52 replied, "All you need to know is Sunny will be the entertainment for the 4th of July event. But, always remember each agent is a part of a team."

The group was quiet, and Inrun52 said, "This meeting is over. Keep up the good work, agents. I have all the faith in the world you will be the best team I have ever supervised."

She added, "Dale, you and Stanley go ahead and leave. The other agents arrived in vans and parked in the garage. I will release them at intervals."

"Cooksey, will you help me to clean the kitchen and counter?"

EPISODE 46

"This is the one. It's perfect," Katherine said. "We can decorate it before you have to report to work today. I took the decorations from storage this morning. The kids will be so excited."

"Did you tell the kids we would bring home a Christmas tree?" Larry asked.

"No, but I told your Dad. I'm sure when he starts rearranging furniture and brings the tree stand out, they will guess," Katherine said with the same smile Larry fell in love with.

Katherine's cell phone rang while Larry was paying for the tree. "Hello."

E. H. said, "I have the speaker on, and two kids want to ask you something."

Katherine and Larry could hear Jordan say, "I'm the oldest, so I talk first."

"It doesn't matter. I'm the sweetest," Skylar said.

The couple heard E. H. take charge as he said, "You both ask them at the same time. One, two, three...Go."

Two voices began yelling, "Are we getting a Christmas tree today?"

Katherine laughed and said, "Your daddy and I will have it there in a little while. We will be bringing burgers and fries for dinner. See you soon. Love you."

E. H. took the phone off of speaker and said to Katherine, "Do you want me to bring the decorations into the family room?"

"No, we will wait until after we eat. I know the children are excited, but they can wait a bit longer. I love you, E. H. You are a blessing to this family." Katherine expressed.

Clearing his throat, E. H. said, "I don't know what I would do without all of you."

EPISODE 47

Dale drove into the parking lot of Edwards Diner, parked, and just sat in his car. He could see a few people sitting at the tables and two people at the bar. This day wasn't the first time he had parked in the restaurant's front without going in.

He did not notice when a truck parked beside him. He just sat there trying to get the nerve to walk in. He had not been inside the restaurant since Pam died. He laid his head back on the headrest.

Katherine was talking to Larry as they parked, and then she saw Dale. Larry, Dale's sitting in his truck, and he's just leaning his head back against the headrest?"

"I saw him parked there last week and came out to talk to him. Dale said he didn't think he could go in, and he drove off when I went back into the restaurant." Larry replied.

She asked, "What do you think about him coming home with us and having dinner?"

"Are you sure? We've always made decorating the tree a family event," answered Larry.

Katherine said, "E. H. if fond of him. Maybe it will help your father. You know how sad he gets when we do family events. He misses your mother so much."

"You are right," said Larry as he opened the truck door.

Dale raised his head from the steering wheel and reached for the starter. He couldn't do it today. Suddenly he noticed someone standing beside his truck door.

He put his window down and looked at Larry with relief. "Still can't do it," he said.

Larry said, "Katherine and I would like for you to come home and eat with us. We just stopped for take-out burgers,"

Dale looked over, and Katherine had put her window down. She waved and said, "Please."

Relief swept over Dale. He couldn't think of anything he had rather do. He just wanted to be with friends, and E. H.'s family was the best. "Yes. Thank you," Dale said, almost in tears.

Dale saw Katherine smile and clap her hands. It reminded him of Skylar when she was excited. He smiled back and said, "Let me buy the food."

Larry reached in and put his hand on Dale's shoulder, and spoke softly, "We want to do this. You go ahead to our home and tell E. H. we will be there soon. Burgers and fries, OK?"

"Yes. I'll see you there," Dale said as he started his truck. He was entirely in a different mood and relieved not to have to go into the restaurant.

EPISODE 48

Vernon had been sitting in Edwards Restaurant when Dale drove up. He saw Dale place his head on the headrest. He assumed Dale had been in love with Pam and was having a hard time accepting her being gone.

Sheriff Maddox thought *I know how he feels. Pearl is gone, and I may never see her again, but at least I can have hope.*

He began eating his meal and noticed Larry Denton and his wife drive up. He saw Larry get out of his truck and talk to Dale. Then Dale left, and Larry walked into the restaurant.

Larry looked at the sheriff, and Vernon nodded towards him. Larry went up to the bar and placed his large order. Larry told the waitress he would be outside in his truck to please come to the window and let him know when the order was ready.

Vernon Maddox was watching all this while he considered the information which Detective Perez gave him. A few weeks earlier, he had asked her to meet him at the office.

On that day, when he closed the door, Vernon could see Perez was confused. Not only was she confused but shocked when Vernon told her he had something personal to ask her and added he would never ask her to do anything outside of the law.

After Detective Perez sat down, Vernon leaned forward and asked her if she could keep a secret. He told her he would like her to find someone in Baltimore, and he would give her some time off and pay her the going rate for private investigators. She had accepted the task and remained attentive as Vernon gave her the information.

As he sat there thinking about how quickly Perez had found his beloved Pearl and their daughter, he was still amazed. He had paid Perez the double rate for an investigator and thanked her. She had thanked him for trusting her and again told him no one else would ever know.

All he had to do now was to get the nerve to contact her. Knowing where Pearl and Verna live makes it painful. As soon as I find the Eight Ball murderer and the person who killed Pam Lawson, Vernon said to himself *I will retire.*

He had no way of knowing all the things that would happen before seeing Pearl's face again.

EPISODE 49

It was an unforgettable weekend. Katherine and Larry had Friday, Saturday, and Sunday off. They decided there would not be a honey-do-list and had spent a good part of Friday in their room talking and making love. E. H. had gotten the children off to school and left the house to spend some time with Martin.

About one o'clock, the couple showered, dressed, and came down to the kitchen. There was a note from E. H. about his visit with Martin. There was a big pot of beef stew on the stove, biscuits in a covered basket, and tea in the refrigerator.

Both of the young lovers worked in unison to heat the stew and biscuits in the microwave. They set the table for themselves, took out the tea, and ate as if they were famished.

After the meal, they cleaned up the kitchen and put the food away. Just as the family was finishing, E. H. walked in and said, "Y'all had a good day?" Before they could answer, Skylar and Jordan were coming in the door while pushing each other.

"I'm telling Mama," Said Jordan.

Skylar shot back, "You are a big tattle tale."

With a slightly raised voice, Katherine said, "Hey. What is going on with you two?"

Quickly Jordan said, "Skylar beat up Johnnell Watson on the playground today."

"I did not," Skylar shouted.

"Yes, you did," Jordan said with his teeth clutched together.

E. H. observed the shouting match as Larry said, "Both of you be quiet."

Katherine said, "Jordan, go to your room and put your books away. Stay there until I call you."

"But, Mama," said Jordan as his mother gave him you-better-do-what-I say-look.

Jordan looked at his dad for help. Larry pointed to the door and said, "Go."

As soon as the door closed, Skylar started crying and talking so fast the words ran together, "Johnnell is a bully, and he said girls couldn't fight. He told me I had ugly red hair and skinny legs."

Skylar caught her breath and began again, "When I told him I did know how to fight, he laughed and called me a baby, so I made two fists and hit him in the belly and the nose."

It was all Katherine could do to keep a smile off her face. She watched as Larry turned his back, trying to hide his feelings.

She looked at her daughter, who was standing still with her chin tilting upward. It was apparent Skylar believed she had defended her honor.

"What happened then?" Katherine asked.

With a broad smile, Skylar said, "He started crying."

Larry cleared his throat to stop the chuckle from leaving his mouth. Katherine wiped her hand across her lips to stop her smiling. She turned to look at E. H, who had his lips pressed together to conceal his smile.

Katherine squatted down in front of Skylar and said, "Skylar, you can't fight because of words people use. Do you remember what Grandma used to say?"

"Yes, Mommy. She told us sticks and stones could break your bones, but words will never hurt you."

"That is right," Katherine said.

"OK, Mommy. I won't hit him again unless he has a stick or a stone. Then I'm going to give him two more fists," Skylar replied.

E. H. walked forward. Katherine saw him and motioned for him to speak to Skylar. He sat on the dining chair and asked Skylar to walk toward him. When she stood in front of him, he said, "Skylar, your grandmother also told you to do unto others as you would want them to do unto you."

"Yes, Grandpa, I remember what she said, but if I called Johnnell names, I would expect him to hit me. And Grandpa, I am not a bully."

Suddenly all three adults realized Skylar was not a baby anymore. She grew to be an intelligent child trying to use the things taught her to solve her problem.

While they were proud, she had learned to take care of herself, and they also realized she would need guidance on how to do it without fighting.

E. H. said gently, "Skylar, we want you to know how to defend yourself, but you have to remember hitting someone is rarely the answer. Remember what your mother and father taught you.

Be kind. Walk away if you have to. Bully's hate for you to walk away, and they may call you other names. Talk to your teachers. It is not a tattle tale. It's a way to help the bully learn different ways to act. You are a sweet girl and beautiful inside and out."

Skylar looked puzzled and asked, "How can you be beautiful on the inside. All those squishy things inside can't be pretty."

All three adults let their laughs escape, and E. H. said, "Being pretty on the inside means your heart. God puts love, gentleness, forgiveness, and understanding in your heart. He gave you those things so you would be a good person even when someone else makes it hard for you to do so. Do you understand?"

"I think so. You want me to be a kind person," answered Skylar.

"Yes, Sweetie, I do."

"I will try, Grandpa."

The Denton family spent the rest of the afternoon playing Chinese checkers. It was E. H.'s favorite board game. He was good at it, so he usually let one of the others win. After the board games, the adults prepared supper and discussed the next day's plan.

The next day the Denton family dressed for the cold weather and went on a nature walk. Everyone enjoyed walking on the farm. E. H. had taken Larry on the same kind of walk while teaching him to appreciate the forest and all its little critters.

Sometimes, if they were lucky, they would walk across the plowed fields and find arrowheads and pieces of pottery the Native Americans left behind. E. H. loved teaching his grandchildren things to pass on to his great-grandchildren.

After supper, Katherine helped Skylar and Jordan put away the clothes she had washed, dried, and folded. Later, when the kids were in bed, Katherine and Larry watched a nature program E. H. had recorded. Larry's radio toned. He rose from his chair to turn it off. Before he did, the operator gave the address.

Larry looked at Katherine inquisitively and said, "It's right down the road."

Katherine's first thought was, *this weekend is ours.* But she said, "Go ahead. It probably won't take long, and first at the scene will give you an idea who else they should call out. Please don't stay long."

Larry walked over and kissed his wife on her forehead and said, "I'll be right back."

When Larry arrived at the scene, he saw smoke coming out of a front window of the old blue and white single-wide trailer.

As he was getting out of the truck, a woman rushed up to him. She was crying and yelling. Larry asked her to calm down.

The wrinkled-face skinny woman cried out, "My baby. My baby. Please get my baby."

"Where is your baby?" Larry asked.

The sobbing woman pointed to the left side of the trailer and said, "Baby is in the bedroom. There is a door on the other side."

Immediately Larry ran towards the back of the old trailer. He reached the door and quickly touched it to see if it was hot. It was not. The woman was standing near the door and cried out, "Hurry."

Larry said, "Get back." He opened the door, and a ball of barking fuzz ran between his legs.

He heard the woman yelling, "Baby, you are safe."

In an instant, the chemical smell hit his nose. He thought, *crack house*, as the trailer exploded into a massive ball of

fire. The explosion knocked the woman and Baby over as the Blackstone County Fire Department pulled into the driveway beside Larry's truck.

EPISODE 50

Stanley watched as Larry's burned body was loaded into the ambulance. It felt like he was walking in a dream. How could this have happened? This victim of the Blackstone County drug fight had come too close to home. Stanley wanted to go after any and everyone who was involved. He was so angry he snapped when Dwight went around the corner of the rescue vehicle.

"What in the hell do you want?" Stanley asked irately.

"It's time to take him in. I have a woman waiting for me." Dwight said nonchalantly.

Dwight didn't notice Stanley had made a fist with his right hand. As Stanley walked toward Dwight, one of the other firefighters walked up and said, "Thanks, guys."

Stanley unclenched his fist and asked, "Has anyone notified his family?"

"Jim and I are on the way," Answered the young man.

Stanley nodded his head in acknowledgment and turned back, and said to Dwight. "Get in and drive. I don't want your whore money to go to waste."

Dwight tensed and started to speak but shrugged his shoulders instead. He got into the truck and drove to the hospital. When he arrived, he told Stanley, "You handle the rest. I have to go."

Stanley was glad to see him leave. After the transfer of the body was made, Stanley cleaned and restocked the ambulance and drove it to the fire station. As he was doing so, he realized he must tell Dale.

As soon as Stanley finished, it was very early Saturday morning; still not light. He got into his vehicle and headed to Dale's apartment. Stanley knocked. Dale came to the door in his sweatpants and without a shirt. When he opened the door, he saw the look on Stanley's face and said, "What happened, Man?"

"Can I come in?" Stanley asked.

Dale stepped to the side, and Stanley walked into the apartment. He went to the small dining table, sat down, and said, "Will you make some coffee?"

Without answering, Dale began the process of making the coffee. He retrieved a cup from the cabinet and put it on the counter.

He knew Stanley usually liked his coffee black. He looked at Stanley again; there was something strange about his facial features.

Stanley sat quietly at the table, watching everything Dale did. Dale went to his dresser, pulled out a sweatshirt, put it on, and walked back to the kitchen area.

He watched the coffee flow slowly into the pot. When it was ready, he poured the coffee into Stanley's cup and sat down; he asked his friend, "What's up, Stanley?"

Stanley looked into the face of his friend and said, "Larry is dead."

Dale said, "What?"

Stanley cleared his throat and said a little louder, "Larry was killed in an explosion."

Dale knew Larry was off for the whole weekend. Stunned, he asked, "What about the rest of the family?"

"They were at home."

Another question from Dale came, "Wasn't Larry off for the weekend?"

Stanley realized why Dale was confused and said, "The fire was close to his house, so he drove over before the firetrucks could get there."

"This isn't funny," said Dale skeptically.

"It's not a joke, Dale. Larry arrived at the trailer as smoke was coming from the windows. A woman was crying about her baby being in the house.

He went inside to get the baby, and the trailer exploded. She was making meth, and it exploded before Larry could get out."

"And the baby?"

Stanley rubbed his hands over his eyes and forehead before answering. "The woman's dog was named Baby. It ran out just before the whole place blew up.

Incredulously Dale asked, "Do you mean Larry lost his life for a dog?"

"Yes."

Dale stood up and said, "I have to see E. H. I've got to go." Dale grabbed his car keys from the counter and headed to the door of the apartment before he realized he was in sweats and barefooted. He looked back at Stanley and said, "I'll shower and get dressed. Will you go with me?"

"I'll wait here. We will go together." Stanley said.

EPISODE 51

When Vernon Maddox, Sheriff of Blackstone County, arrived at the Sheriff Department at six o'clock in the morning, the parking lot was more crowded than it should have been on a Saturday.

He wondered what could have happened and why so many deputies were at the station.

Vernon looked around when he went inside and saw several deputies in a group talking in soft voices. Everyone looked somber.

When Vernon saw Perez, she had been crying. He continued to walk towards his office. Everyone stopped and watched Vernon walk into his office and close the door. He turned and looked out at the others questioning in his mind, *what in the hell has everyone so upset.*

He walked to his door, opened it, and stood in the doorway as he asked, "Will someone tell me what is going on?"

The deputies and detectives looked dumbfounded. They just stood looking, and no one spoke. Vernon called out, "Perez, come in here now."

Everyone looked at Perez as she walked toward Vernon's office. Vernon stepped out of her way as she came into the room. He walked around his desk and sat down. "Sit down, Perez, and tell me what is going on."

Perez sniffed as she said, "We thought you knew."

"Knew what?" demanded the Sheriff.

"Larry Denton was killed last night."

Bewildered, he said, "The son of E. H. Denton?"

"Yes. There was an explosion at a trailer near where Larry lives...I mean lived."

"Perez, can you tell me the whole story without me having to pull it out of you?" He said in a cantankerous manner.

When Perez finished telling him the whole story, he stood up and walked out of his office, through the gantlet of stares, and out the door of the building.

As his thoughts simmered, he said to himself, *this time you have hurt a good family.*

He headed to see E. H. Denton and his family. He felt culpable and had no idea what he was going to say. However, he did know Blackstone County would never be the same. He would stop what had gotten out of hand. He didn't know how; he only knew he had to do something.

EPISODE 52

Six firemen carried the flag-draped casket down the church steps as E. H., Katherine, Jordan, and Skylar followed. Firefighters lined the sidewalk, many from other towns. As the six firemen carrying the casket approached the old fire truck, the other people began filing from the church. They placed the coffin on the fire truck, and the immediate family ushered to an awaiting car.

The fire truck and the Cadillac waited until the other attendees were in their vehicle, and then they began the drive to the cemetery.

The lights on the fire truck blinked as if going to an emergency. The headlight on each car, shown for respect.

As the vehicles approached oncoming automobiles, as a Southern tradition to show respect, the owners pulled to the side of the road and stopped until the whole procession had passed.

At the cemetery, the casket laid on the brass holders above the grave. Larry's family and friends sat under a tent, waiting for the others to get out of their vehicles and gather around the grave.

When all was still and quiet, a tone came from one of a firemen's radio. It seemed no one breathed as the county dispatcher called out for Larry Harold Denton.

Twice more, the tone sounded the call for Larry. When the third call received no answer, the fire station attendant said, "No response from Larry Harold Denton.

Larry, your service has been valuable and honorable, and we thank you. We relieve you from the worldly calls and release you to your rightful place with the Lord."

After the last call, the only sounds were sniffles and blowing of noses. The first to move was the firemen who took the American flag from the casket and then folded it. When the Fire Chief handed the flag to Katherine, she broke down for a few seconds.

Before lowering the casket into the grave, Katherine stood and walked over to the coffin. She kissed the daisy she held and began to remove the petals and dropped each one on the casket while saying, "He loves me, he loves me not," until one last petal remained.

She pulled it off and laid it with the others, and said, "He loves me." She laid the remaining part of the daisy with the petals which lay on the casket and bent to kiss the casket.

At which point, the children walked over to their mother. Katherine nodded to Jordan. He then placed a picture he had drawn of him and his daddy playing catch. He kissed the casket also. Skylar pulled at her mother's hand, saying, "Is it my turn?"

Katherine whispered, "Yes, as she picked her up and leaned her towards the casket as Skylar said, "Here, Daddy. I am giving you is my favorite hair ribbon of all the ones I have. I know you liked to see them in my hair.

Keep this one, and don't forget me because Mommy said we would see you in heaven one day. I'll be all grown up by then."

After Katherine and the children sat down, E. H. stood and walked to the casket. He did not say a word. He began taking things out of his jacket pocket and placed each on the coffin. The first was a tiny toy fire truck, then a small red tractor, and lastly, a small fishing pole with a realistic fish on the end of the line. E. H. began to sink to his knees as sobs broke from his shaking body.

Everyone stood in place until E. H. regained control and sat back down. The firemen began to file by the family.

Next, the crowd slowly approached and filed by E. H., Katherine, Jordan, and Skylar as they softly gave condolences. The four sat in the chairs even after the crowd began to walk to their cars.

Katherine turned her gaze away from the casket to see several of Larry's and her classmates standing in a group. She got up and walked towards them. She recognized them all except one, but she quickly realized Sunny was in one of her disguises.

They all gathered around her for a group hug. Katherine told them how much it meant to her for them to come. She knew Sunny was not the only one to travel a long distance, and she appreciated their show of love for her and her family. Even with the sadness, she felt they managed to smile with a few stories of their relationship with Larry.

In a few moments, Katherine heard Skylar calling as she ran towards her mother. Katherine looked past Skylar and saw E. H. standing a few feet away, holding Jordan's hand.

She turned to her group of friends and thanked them again as Skylar took her hand, asking, "Who are all these people, Mama."

"They are high school friends of your daddy," Katherine answered. "They came to honor your daddy."

"Oh." Said Skylar, and she began to pull on Katherine's sleeve, "Mama, Mama, Mama, Granddaddy is ready to leave. He wants to go home. He is so sad."

The group took the signal, and each gave Katherine a little hug or a kiss and walked away. The last one to leave was Sunny.

She stood until all the others were gone and then said, "Katherine, if you ever need anything, please call me on the private number. Don't forget...anything." She then placed a hand on Katherine's cheek and brushed a kiss on the other cheek. She turned and walked away to the limousine which was waiting for the bereaved family.

Katherine and Skylar walked towards Jordan and her father-in-law to begin life without Larry. She could not imagine what kind of life it would be. Larry had always been in her life, even before she was born.

EPISODE 53

When Dwight Gacy drove into the driveway of Sheriff Maddox's house, he saw Junior Maddox's Jaguar. He got out of his truck and held onto his keys. Dwight wanted to walk by Junior's car and key it down the side, deep. He smiled at the thought, but he knew better. It was not worth being killed.

Dwight walked up the steps and saw Junior standing behind the screen door. Junior did not look happy. As Junior opened the door, he stepped aside. Dwight walked into the kitchen as the screen door slammed. He turned and faced Junior.

"Sit down, Dwight," Junior ordered. "We need to talk."

"Sure, Boss. Got a beer?" said Dwight with a smug look.

Junior opened the frig, took out two beers, and sat one down in front of Dwight so hard it could have broken. He sat down across from Dwight, opened his beer, drank half of it, set it down, and cupped his hands around the bottle.

Junior knew Dwight believed himself to be cunning and clever. He stared at him until he began to squirm in his chair.

Junior drank the rest of his beer and threw the bottle across the room. It hit the wall when the bottle shattered. Junior could see Dwight become tense.

"What's wrong, Dwight? Are you getting jumpy in your old age?" Junior asked.

Dwight cocked his head at an angle, put his chin up, and said, "I ain't old. I am just waiting to hear why you wanted to see me."

"What have you been doing with your spare time, Old Man?" Junior asked in a silky but threatening voice.

Dwight usually did not let anyone bully him, but Junior Maddox was not just anyone, and Junior paid him a lot of money to look the other way, "What do you mean, boss. I do my job and have ears listening for things you need to know."

"Since your ears have been listening, what do you know about the Eight Ball killer? And, who killed that waitress, Pam?" Junior asked.

Not giving Dwight time to answer, he continued saying, "Two detectives are looking into the Eight Ball killings, and now they are trying to find out who is responsible for the meth house which blew up.

You do know Larry Denton was well-liked by everyone and never bothered anyone...if you know what I mean."

Dwight hoped he looked as cool as a cucumber on the outside; however, he was in turmoil on the inside. He managed a smile when he said, "Boss, I've been asking a lot of questions.

The Eight Ball killer is like a ghost. He strikes and is gone. He leaves no clues. I think he is the same one who killed the waitress, but I don't know any more than the detectives. Nobody is talking."

Pausing to look for clues in Junior's attitude, Dwight took a swallow of his beer. He put it down, leaned back in the kitchen chair, and said, "The word on the street is the old woman with the dog was cooking meth for a few people in the trailer park to make a little extra money."

Dwight watched Junior get up, walk to the frig, get another beer, sit back down and open it before saying, "If I find out you are lying to me or you know more than you are telling, I'm going to plant you in one of my azalea gardens at the Stonehouse Farm. You will make good fertilizer, just like manure."

"I told you what I know," Dwight said.

"You know what is coming up in a few weeks. Don't do anything which will cause problems. Do you understand?" Junior Maddox threatened.

"Yes, Boss, I understand." Dwight answered and added, "The New Year's Eve party went off without a hitch, and I'm sure your Caesar shindig will blow them away."

When Dwight stood up, Junior walked over to him and punched his finger into Dwight's chest with every word as he said, "You are disposable, so don't cross me."

It was a cold day, but Dwight Gacy walked out of the Maddox house with sweat circles under his arms. More than before, Dwight wanted to key Junior Maddox's fancy car.

What he didn't know was while he was talking to Junior, Dwight's vehicle received a GPS tracker, a listening device, and a small camera inside the air vent.

Dwight got into his car. He was furious with Junior and surmised *Junior has no right to judge me; he bumps off people all the time.*

His hand went to his chest where Junior had poked his finger six times.

While backing out of the driveway, he thought, *I need to go huntin' and have a little fun; it's a shame I only have to settle for a hooker.*

EPISODE 54

Katherine Denton lay in her upstairs bedroom of the old 17th century home. She was tossing and turning, whimpering, and whispering.

In a few moments, she began breathing hard and in seconds was softly laughing like a child with a new puppy. In a few more seconds, she said, "You too."

Katherine suddenly opened her eyes. Once she did, the laughter stopped, and tears began. The memory of making love with Larry had been so real. She could hear Larry laughing as he rolled to his side. Then he put his hand on her belly and snuggled against her neck.

It was the way they always ended their lovemaking. He would tell her he loved her, and she would say, "you too." Both would quickly fall asleep.

She hugged herself as the silent tears turned into sobs. It had been only a few weeks since Larry died. She had experienced similar dreams, but this was the first one where she and Larry shared the lovemaking before she awoke.

Now the loneliness and loss of her husband were more poignant than ever. Katherine lay there until the sobs subsided. She turned towards the clock to see how much longer it would be before daylight.

It was only three, and she felt she could not sleep anymore, but she did. The clock went off at six-thirty. She thought, *another day to get through and another night to dream.*

EPISODE 55

Dale had buried himself in his work at the garage for several days. He knew he needed to visit E. H., but each morning he made an excuse for himself and tried to work mindlessly.

He didn't want to think about his brother, Rex, his little sister, Pam, or about his good friend, Larry. In a few months, three of his friends had lost their lives, and he had lost people who were like family. He had talked to Stanley a couple of times but declined his invitation to go out to eat.

Dale finished the truck he was working on and slammed the hood so hard it sounded like a gunshot. Rodney came out of his art shop to see what happened.

"Hey man, are you OK?" Rodney asked.

"Yeah, sorry, Rodney," Dale said right before he sat on the floor and leaned back on the truck tire. He wanted to yell at someone or something, but all he could do was sob.

Mozart stayed very close to Dale for weeks; since Larry's and Pam's death. He put his head on Dale's leg and stayed until Dale felt like standing again.

Rodney wanted to do something to make Dale feel better. Since they both found out they were agents for Inrun52; they had avoided talking about it.

You never knew who the bad guys were. However, he and Dale knew Junior Maddox was a very, bad guy and unknowingly, they both had the same thoughts. They wanted him to pay.

Once Dale got himself together, he realized it was past lunchtime, and he had not eaten breakfast. As he headed to his apartment, Junior Maddox began banging on the door to the art shop.

Mozart began to growl as Dale stopped without turning around. His hands went into a tight fist. He just wanted to hit Junior, but he couldn't. Rodney was probably working on another false dashboard or something similar. Dale was glad the time grew nearer every day.

Dale leaned to pat his dog and said, "Mozart, you are a good dog-friend, and that Maddox man isn't worth getting in trouble for."

After lunch, Dale called Stanley and asked Stanley if he had seen E. H. He said he had not, so they decided to talk with him that afternoon.

The visit had been emotional for all three men, but Dale felt much better afterward. E. H. was like a father to him, and Dale knew they needed each other more than ever.

As he drove home, he thought about the few months he had left to spend with E. H. and Stanley. He would make the most of it.

Immediately Katherine came to mind, but he scolded himself, saying she just lost her husband and would never want me. I won't be here much longer anyway.

EPISODE 56

As Sheriff Vernon Maddox, several of his detectives, and officers were going over the lack of progress on the Eight Ball murderer, Dwight Gacy was home thinking how much he missed his fun times. He was off for two days, and he began making his plan.

Dwight lived in the garage of his grandmother's home. He had happily moved in with her almost ten years ago when she was going through chemotherapy. He knew she would die soon, and he would be the one getting her house.

She had proved him wrong. After fourteen months of treatment, she was declared cancer-free and had been going strong since receiving the good news. She was more robust and healthier than ever because she exercised with her friends and ate differently.

Mrs. Casey was a kind and soft-spoken, church-going woman. She constantly worried about her grandson and prayed for him fervently.

She constantly tried to get him to go to church socials and anywhere else to make friends or find a nice girl. She worried because he never had friends coming over and believed him to be an unfortunate, lonely man.

Dwight constantly asked her to stop nagging since he saw her concern and care as such. He assumed she only wanted to make his life miserable.

It was the reason he moved out of the extra bedroom and had created a man cave in the garage. He heated the garage with a small electric heater in the winter and had no air conditioning in the warmer months.

When he moved into the garage, he purchased a big screen TV with cable hookup, a refrigerator that usually contained only beer. He bought a coffee maker, a microwave, and a composting toilet.

When Dwight's father built the house, a 'work' sink was installed for garage use, but Dwight used cold water to make coffee, bathing, and shaving. He also purchased an oversized comfortable couch which he used to sit and to sleep.

Dwight had three uniforms, two pairs of jeans, three shirts, seven pairs of socks, five pairs of underwear, work boots, cowboy boots, and one heavy coat for the winter.

When he needed clothes washed, he carried them into the house and threw them on the floor in front of the washing machine.

Sometimes his grandmother would enter while he was gone to gather the items she deemed needed washing. When Dwight would get home the next day, they would be in a cardboard box in the garage.

Sometimes his grandmother would leave prepared food in the refrigerator in throw-away containers. She quickly learned her grandson would throw away dishes, pots, or tableware after eating the food. So, she also supplied him with plastic utensils, a throw-away coffee cup, paper towels, and paper plates.

Dwight rarely went into the house, and if he did, it would be while Mrs. Gacy was at church. Sometimes they did not see each other for weeks, but it did not stop her from inviting him to eat with her. He never did, not on Christmas or Thanksgiving.

While Dwight was mulling his plans over in his mind, he fell asleep. When he woke up three hours later, he could hear voices through the walls. His grandmother had company again. He took off his uniform and let it lay where it dropped. He put on a clean shirt, jeans, and cowboy boots. He then drank a beer, got his truck key, and walked out the door. He was going hunting.

EPISODE 57

It was five o'clock AM when Junior Maddox's cell phone rang out with the musical theme from the 1950's TV show, Dragnet. He looked at the caller and answered, "This better be damn important."

His caller was talking so fast Junior could barely understand the conversation, "He's done it again, Boss."

Irritated, Junior asked, "Who did what?"

"The Eight Ball killer...He's done it again."

"Where?"

"They found a girl near Roseville thrown off a bridge. A late-night fisherman was fishing for catfish nearby, and he saw a man in a pickup truck throw the girl off the bridge."

"Another hooker?"

"Not this time, boss; a nice college girl. She *weren't* but twenty-two. He left her car in the mall parking lot with a flat tire. Her phone and purse were by the car."

"Holy crap! Was it him?"

"The computer stuff you had me install got it all, boss. He was parked there at a Raleigh mall. The video showed him putting her into the truck. Then he drove to a motel.

Later he put her back in the truck without her clothes and drove to the bridge. He took her out, threw her over the bridge rail, and he went home."

"Where is he now?"

"He's at his grandma's in the garage. What do you want me to do?"

"Bring him to the Stonehouse. I'll be there in an hour. Do not let him out of your sight."

"Yes, Sir, Boss. He will be there."

It was the first time Dwight hunted in Raleigh. He knew the places the hooker hung out, but he wanted something different. He wanted one of those nice girls his grandma always said he needed.

He drove around until he was near one of the many small shopping centers in the area. He turned in and began riding around, looking for the parking lot cameras. He had to find a place where no one could see him. He finally saw a parking spot where an overgrown cedar tree blocked the camera view.

Dwight Gacy's conversation with Junior Maddox had infuriated him, and he was letting his anger drive him. His excitement of the hunt for a nice girl soothed his mental lesions, and the hunger for relief made him careless.

He watched the people getting in and out of their cars for over an hour. He was like a crocodile waiting just beneath the water, watching for his pray.

A car pulled away, which parked to the right of Dwight, and immediately another pulled in. The girl who got out of the car caught his eye immediately.

Dwight's new pray had long blond hair pulled into a ponytail, and she appeared to wear no makeup, wore jeans and a white T-shirt with Micky Mouse on the front.

After she closed her door and put her key into her purse, she turned and smiled at Dwight. He smiled back and nodded his head. She continued her walk to the mall.

The hunter got out of his truck, walked to the truck bed, and reached into a toolbox. He pulled out an ice pick and looked around. No one was in the area, so he walked to the driver's side of the girl's car, punctured the rear tire, and put the ice pick back into his toolbox.

He looked around and began to walk to the door of the mall where the girl had entered. He stood there for over two hours, waiting.

When he saw her walk out, he followed a few feet behind and arrived just in time to see the girl notice her flat tire. He walked towards her and said, "Wow, that is bad luck, young lady. Can I help?"

"No, I'll call someone. Thanks, though," The young blond answered.

"I have a jack in my truck. I can have it changed in five minutes, and I have not done my good deed for the day," He said and added, "How about helping with my promise to my mama. I told her I would do one good deed every day." He began putting on a pair of work gloves.

The pretty young girl smiled and put her phone back into her purse. "Well, I guess it will be alright." She then handed her key to Dwight and said, "The spare is in the trunk."

He dropped her keys, and when she bent down to get them, he quickly looked around. No one was close enough to notice when he took the chloroform-laden rag out of his pocket and held it over her face. She went limp. Instead of picking her up, he dragged her around to his truck, opened his door, and pulled her up. Dwight shoved her across to the passenger seat.

Dwight Gacy started his truck and began singing with the radio. He drove to the outskirts of Raleigh to a motel he sometimes took hookers for sex. However, this time Dwight wasn't after only sex. He was after the rush he felt when he became the Eight Ball killer.

After Dwight tied and gaged his nice girl, he sat and waited until she began to wake up. He turned the TV up and started the process. When done and she was dead, it was late.

She was undressed when he put her in the truck beside him. He admired his art as he headed for a seldom traveled road a few miles from Roseville.

When he came to the bridge, he took her out and dropped her over the bridge rail. Dwight took his rubber gloves off and stuck them into his pocket with the young girl's panties and the condom he used. He headed home.

EPISODE 58

Within an hour, Junior was walking into the back door of the Stonehouse. When he saw his man, he said, "Where is he?"

"He's down in Barn B. He's tied up and hung by his legs like a deer waiting to be skinned and chopped up. I put some plastic on the barn floor just in case. He is yelling a lot, Boss. What do you aim to do with him?"

"Who else is on the farm today?" Junior asked.

"Just old Cotton, Boss. He ain't gonna do nothing."

"Come on. I'm going to talk to the Eight Ball killer."

Dressed in a suit and a white shirt with the collar unbuttoned and no tie, Junior tilted his chin upward and sniffed the farm air.

Junior Maddox's shoes were shined and then scuffed to make him look more like a working man. He looked at the man who had helped him make people disappear, cleared his throat, and said, "Come with me; this will be fun. The man followed Junior to the barn.

When Junior walked in, Dwight spits out curse words Junior had never heard before. Junior walked around the hanging man without saying a word. Dwight's arms, tied to the waist. He spat at Junior.

When Junior stopped walking, he stood there until Dwight quit yelling. He said, "What were you doing last night, Mad Dog."

"I went to Raleigh, found me a hooker, and we screwed a couple of hours. Then I came home."

Very calmly, Junior asked, "Did this hooker happen to be a pretty little college girl with a flat tire."

Junior could see terror go across Dwight's face. He continued with the same calm and soft voice, "Did you throw her off a bridge near Roseville, Dwight?"

Dwight's face was flushed with blood from hanging upside down, but Junior could see his skin turn pale and beads of water pop from his pores.

Junior asked, "What do you think I should do to you, Dwight Gacy?"

Dwight just stared at the barn wall as he peed and crapped his pants. He knew he was doomed. Junior moved, and Dwight turned to look at him.

Junior said, "What did I tell you I would do if I found out you were the Eight Ball murderer? And yes, I put a tracker and a tiny little camera in your truck, Dwight. Wasn't that clever of me?

Dwight did not speak, but his eyes followed Junior's moves. Junior reached his hand out to The-Man and said, "Where is it?

Junior's man walked out the door, came back with a hunting knife, and handed it to Junior. He turned his back to what was about to happen. Dwight closed his eyes and whimpered. Junior took the knife and slit Dwight's throat.

Junior told his man what to do, and then he left. The grinning man took a back-hoe from the farm shelter and went to the woods to dig a big hole.

When he finished, he put Dwight and the plastic sheet into a back-hoe bucket and carried him to the grave.

He dropped Dwight in and then filled the hole. After he packed the dirt, he picked up straw, leaves, and twigs and sprinkled them around until the whole area looked natural.

He returned the back-hoe to the shelter. He removed his work gloves and put on surgical gloves before taking the USB thumb drive from the laptop computer. He wiped the drive clean of fingerprints

He took the hard drive from the computer and pounded the laptop with a hammer until it broke into several pieces. He then placed the hard drive and the computer parts into a five-gallon bucket containing a mixture of nail polish remover and salt. He sat it in the corner of the shelter.

The last thing Junior Maddox ordered to do was drop a flash drive into the back of Dwight's pick-up. Later he would remove the part's from the bucket, drain, bag and carry it to the county waste station.

EPISODE 59

Vernon Maddox pulled into E. H. Denton's driveway. It was mid-morning, and he didn't want to go to the Office. He had felt compelled to visit E. H.

He dropped by a couple of times to talk with E. H. since Larry died. All the years he had been in Blackstone County, he had not associated with people on a personal basis. However, E. H., even in his grief, made Vernon feel as if he was an old friend.

When he drove up, he saw E. H. walking across the yard. He got out of his patrol car and walked towards him with his hand out. "Morning, Sir, how are you doing today?" Vernon also spoke to Ratchet, who was wagging his tail.

As E. H. shook the sheriff's hand, he said, "Trying to make it one day at a time. What brings you out today?"

"I thought I would stop by and see how everyone is doing, and honestly, I needed a break from sheriffing," Vernon replied.

"We all need a break from responsibility once in a while. I am going to walk to Blackstone and check on the ancient spirits. Come walk with me," E. H. responded.

Vernon's shoulders pulled out of the slight sag which had plagued him all morning. He gave E. H. a huge smile and said, "Thanks. I've not seen Blackstone since I was a boy."

E. H. laughed and said, "It's still in the same place." E. H. gave the nod to the well-worn path, and they began their walk in the May sunshine.

They walked without speaking for a while. E. H. used walks to clear his mind and refresh his body. After about ten minutes, Vernon said, "Been a long time since I was out in the fresh air and walked just to be walking. It reminds me of when I was a boy and walked down a long path to go fishing."

"Time rushes by," Said E. H. and added, "I walk this trail every day come rain or shine. It never gets old. God provides me new sights every time. It's nothing like it."

Vernon was quiet for a few moments. He was struggling with how to word his question. Finally, he said, "I hear you are a man of God, and if someone needs to talk, you don't judge."

"It's not my place to judge, Vernon. If God wants to use me as his ears, I feel privileged to listen."

The two men rounded the corner in silence. Suddenly the boulder was ahead. Excitedly Vernon said, "It's bigger than I remember. It's something about how the boulder towers over the trees. It makes a man feel rather small."

"Yeah, God has a way of putting things in perspective. The huge granite stone has seen a lot of people come and go," Replied E. H. "Sit down here and rest your back on Blackstone. It soaks in the warmth of the sun and can ease a man's back and his mind."

Both men sat down and leaned against Blackstone. They were quiet for a few minutes, and then Vernon said, "I am thinking about retiring soon. I want to see the Eight Ball killer and Pam Larson's murder solved first. I hate to leave them for a new sheriff."

E. H. waited to see what else Vernon would say and when he didn't speak for a while, E. H. said, "Hate to see you go, but I understand a man has to have some time in life for himself if he lives long enough. What do you plan to do afterward?"

In his mind, Vernon was thinking about how to tell him about Pearl and their daughter. He said, "I want to move away, E. H. I have someone I want to travel with and see a little of our Country."

E. H. had heard all the rumors about Vernon's housekeeper, Pearl, but he only said, "Sounds like you are planning for some happier days ahead. I hope it all works out for you."

Vernon was quiet again. He saw himself, Pearl, and their daughter, standing beside the Grand Canyon. Jokingly, he said, "Might even get married."

While E. H. was thinking of a reply, Vernon's cell phone rang. He gave a grumpy hello and then said, "Where did they find her? OK, I will be there as soon as I can. Who is in the office? Call Perez and Cain to come in. I don't care where they are. Just get them in.

Vernon stood up and said, "I'm sorry, E. H., there has been another Eight Ball murder; got to get to the office."

The incline of the path leaving Blackstone continued until the yard of the Denton home place. The two men briskly walked as Vernon breathed harder and harder.

E. H. was worried Vernon might not make it back to his car, but he did. He left the Denton place with the sirens going and the blue lights flashing.

When Vernon Maddox arrived at the Sheriff's station, he rushed inside and to his office. As soon as he sat down, Detectives Perez and Cain came in.

"Tell me all you know about this murder." Sheriff Maddox demanded.

Detection Cain said, "A call came in from Wake County about thirty minutes ago. The detective there said the woman killed was a twenty-two-year-old college student."

"She was abducted from the Johnson Creek Mall and dumped off Road 1973 near Roseville. A fisherman who was there said a man in a pick-up truck threw her over the rails. It was dark, and the informant was too far away to identify the person or the type of truck."

Vernon asked, "Were there cameras in the mall parking lot?"

"Yes, there are. The Wake detective said the truck driver parked in the only place where the camera did not reach. An overhanging tree hid the perp, and he backed into space."

"They do know it was an older model red truck, maybe an early sixties Ford. They are checking more cameras to see if the murderer got out of the vehicle and went inside," answered Detective Perez.

Suddenly a deputy stood in the doorway and said, "Sheriff, the Wake County detective is on the phone. He wants to talk to you."

Sheriff Maddox picked up the phone and said, "Hello, Sheriff Maddox here." He listened and gave the caller his department email address and said, "Thank you. We will get right back to you."

Detectives Cain and Perez were leaning forward, waiting to hear the information. Vernon looked at them and smiled, "They found a picture of the perp hanging around the door of the mall. It is the same door the young woman used. They are sending those pics and the one showing the perp driving away."

The two detectives and the sheriff sat quietly, waiting for the pictures. Less than a minute later, Vernon's computer made a tiny dinging sound. He quickly opened the email. He promptly said, "Damn, I knew it."

The officers in the room crowded around Vernon's office door. Vernon turned the computer screen so Cain and Perez and the others could see the pictures. Both the detectives leaned closer to the screen; suddenly, Detective Cain sat back down and said, "My god, it's Dwight Gacy."

Vernon yelled, "Take a deputy with you and go pick the bastard up." Everyone in the department heard their sheriff, and more than one officer wanted to go.

EPISODE 60

Dale looked at the clock which hung above his workbench. He had skipped breakfast and was famished. He went to the cleaning station and began getting the grease off his hands while deciding if he wanted beans in his apartment or go to Simon's Food Bar. Unexpectedly Rodney came running out of his art shop and toward Dale.

"What's going on," asked Dale.

Rodney was so excited he was stumbling over his words. He stopped, took a deep breath, and said, "Got a call. They are looking for Dwight Gacy for the Eight Ball murders."

Dale said, "I got to call Stanley."

Oddly Mozart was wagging his tail as if he knew what the two men said. Rodney stood there while Dale called Stanley, and when he answered, he put him on speakerphone. Dale said, "Did you hear about Dwight?"

Stanley said, "Yeah, I can't believe it. I know he is a loudmouth troublemaker, but I had no idea he was a murderer. How did you hear?" Stanley asked.

"Someone called Rodney. He's right here, and I have you on speaker. Is Dwight working today?"

"No. Dwight had three days off. Emergency services called me a few minutes ago and said he wasn't answering his phone. They wanted to know if I knew where he was," said Stanley.

"Do you want to meet me at Simon's Food Bar?" Dale asked.

"Sure. Leaving right now," Stanley said.

Dale's phone went dead. He turned to Rodney and said, "Do you want to eat with us?"

"No, I need to stay here. Let me know if you hear any more news about Dwight, and I'll do the same," replied Rodney. Mozart looked up at Rodney as if to say; I'll stay here with you.

EPISODE 61

When Katherine came in the door, E. H. looked up. She looked tired, so he said, "Sit down with me a few minutes. I'll make you a glass of tea. The kids are playing in Jordan's room. They've been excellent since they came home from school."

Katherine smiled and said, "I'm going to take you up on that. It's been a rough day. We lost two overdosed kids today. One was nineteen, and the other was only fifteen.

It was heroin remixed with fentanyl. Another came in last night with the same tox. He was DOA five minutes after the paramedics arrived."

"How many overdosed this week?" E. H. Asked.

"Seven and all the hospitals within a hundred-mile radius are reporting more cases every day. The kids don't have a chance. Somebody knows it is happening, but all the sellers care about is the money," Katherine said.

E. H. said, "There were several military veterans at the church meeting last night. They are frightened for their comrades who have a drug problem.

They said most of the fentanyl pills the dealers were crushing into powder and sold on the internet. Thousands of fentanyl doses can fit in a small shoebox. Some are selling the non-pharmaceutical drugs out of their sunglasses case so they are easily hidden and transported."

Katherine changed the subject by asking, "Have they found Dwight Gacy?

E. H. hated to tell her what was on the news at five o'clock, but he said, "They received all the DNA reports on the eight pair of panties which found in Dwight's room."

E. H. hesitated again, and Katherine said, "One of them was Pam's, wasn't it?"

"Yes, the other seven were from the girls found dumped from bridges. No one has found the ones the college girl wore. They believed Dwight must still have them with him." E. H. replied.

"Have you heard from Dale?" Katherine asked.

"No. Not yet."

Katherine said, "There is a rumor going around the hospital saying a USB drive found in Dwight's truck showed him taking the girl from the mall."

Shaking his head in agreement, E. H. said, "I've heard the rumor too. I hope this puts the Eight Ball murders to rest," and added, "I'll make some dinner. Now, go hug your kids. You need a distraction."

Katherine managed a laugh and replied, "I can always count on them for a distraction. Thank you so much for all you do. I don't know what I would do without you."

"Same here, Daughter."

EPISODE 62

Dale was still adjusting from the realization Dwight killed Pam. There was a nationwide search for him. No one had seen him since the video of Dwight's last victim.

His mother had heard his old truck when he came home. She had said she always waited up until he came home no matter the time.

After the truck pulled into the driveway, she fell asleep and didn't wake until eight o'clock.

No one else could confirm her story except the poor man across the street in the first stages of Alzheimer's.

There was no need for a search warrant. Dwight's mother didn't deny entry into Dwight's lair. She had no idea her son kept souvenirs of the women he had raped and murdered.

Dwight hid eight pairs of panties almost in the open. They sat on the top of the refrigerator in a cookie jar shaped like an eight ball. His mother was too short of reaching it, so evidently, Dwight deemed it safe.

The panties of the murdered women checked for DNA happened in record time. The NC State Crime Lab had made it a priority, and when Sheriff Vernon Maddox saw the report, he breathed a sigh of relief.

He walked out into the open office area to let everyone know Pam's murder was by Dwight Gacy, the Eight Ball killer.

The room exploded with hand-clapping but only for a few seconds. The gravity of what they had just heard soaked in, and they stopped clapping.

Immediately, Vernon said, "I want to thank every one of you for the extra time you spent helping to close this case. We all worked with Dwight at some point, but I want to add thousands of emergency workers in this state who often risk their lives to save someone else.

Dwight happened to be one rotten apple in a huge barrel. The Sheriff turned and walked into his office and began constructing a retirement request.

The best part of the day was a letter from Pearl. She had just said she loved him, and she and Verna would be waiting until they saw him drive up. The timing was perfect, and Vernon had felt the same as when he was a kid and caught his first fly ball.

EPISODE 63

As Katherine sat down, she realized E.H. was tapping his fingers on the table. A memory flashed across her mind as she thought, *Larry did the same thing when he wanted to have a serious talk.* She felt chill bumps run down her arms.

Before she could think of anything to say, E.H. said, "You look tired."

"Yes. Today was a busy day in the emergency room. Several cases of measles happened at the Stonehope elementary school. Several parents who don't have a family physician came in to have their child checked."

E.H. started tapping again. He pushed his thin white hair from his forehead as he said, "Katherine, you were the best wife for Larry. You made him happy every day, and I couldn't have asked for a better daughter-in-law or a better mother to my grandchildren."

Katherine looked at her father-in-law with puzzlement. "Thank you, E.H.; it makes me feel good, and you know I love you like my own father."

I've felt you did, and I know how hard these last months have been for you. We both suffered a significant loss. "Katherine, I want you to know you can talk to me about anything that is bothering you."

"Sure. I know."

"Well, Sugar, I guess I will just have to come right out with it. I heard something the other day, and I want to talk about it. I'm not upset or angry. I just think we need to talk about it."

"What is it, E.H.?"

"I heard Junior Maddox asked you out several times."

"That's true."

"Why haven't you said yes?"

"I don't believe I am ready," said Katherine. She looked at E.H. as tears flowed down her cheeks. "I miss Larry so much, and I feel I would be dishonoring his memory."

E.H. sniffed and pulled out his handkerchief. He blew his nose and spoke hoarsely, "You are a good woman Katherine, and you are young. I don't expect you to be alone for the rest of your life. You need to get out a bit and have a little fun. Just be true to yourself and remember how your folks raised you."

Katherine said, "You don't have to worry. I want you to always think of me as a fine person and proud to call me the mother of your grandchildren."

E. H. said in a fatherly voice, "Please do one thing. If you are going out with someone, please have him pick you up here. I like the old fashion way."

Katherine replied as E. H. stood up and poured his cup of coffee into the sink, and placed the cup in the dishwasher. "It may be old-fashioned, but I feel the same way, and it will not be anytime soon. I'm not even remotely ready to date.

E. H. said, "Just let me know if you decide to go out with someone. I will keep the children." Then he smiled and said, "Good night, Dear. See you in the morning."

"Thanks, E. H., love you," She said.

Katherine sat at the table and finished her tea. She put the dishes in the dishwasher and turned them on. Katherine felt more relaxed than when she first came home.

She also was happy E.H. brought up the question about going out with Junior. She was relieved it was out in the open, but she wondered who told E.H. She went to sleep with the question running through her head, but she dreamed of Larry.

EPISODE 64

E. H. had told Dale he could walk down the path towards Blackstone anytime, and he didn't have to stop and ask. Dale parked his truck in Denton's yard, got out, and observed the unfamiliar SUV parked in the yard.

Thinking E. H. had visitors; Dale headed for the path to Blackstone. The walk always gave him comfort and helped to clear his mind. Even though the way was familiar, he walked with a flashlight

When he came to the turn in the path, he stopped. He thought he heard voices, so he turned off the flashlight and stood still. He recognized the noise of a deer running through the woods, but he still could hear voices.

Dale smiled when he heard her voice; it was Katherine. He took another step; he listened to another voice. Dale's smile vanished. It was the voice of Junior Maddox.

Dale stopped as Katherine spoke again.

"What are you doing?" Katherine asked.

"Come on, Katherine. I asked you to date me several times. I know you must need a kiss," said Junior.

Katherine spoke angrily, "I told you I am not ready to date."

Junior seductively said, "It's been a while, and you know you are ready for kisses and more. You need 'to get with the new times.' A woman like you must have needs." He grabbed her arm and said, "Let's experiment with one little kiss."

"Yelling, Katherine said, "Let go of my arm."

The rest of what Katherine said sounded muffled, and Dale wanted to stop what seemed to be going on. He was tensing up but decided to wait and see if Katherine could handle it.

Junior said, "I know you must want sex as much as I do. I don't want a relationship."

With a more robust voice, Katherine said, "Go away; leave me alone.

Using his best sexy voice, Junior continued, "I've wanted you since you were in the eighth grade. You are not fooling me. I know you want me. You have been a widow for a while, and I know you need what I can give you."

"I do not," sobbed Katherine.

Dale turned the flashlight on and started walking quickly towards the voices. As he grew closer, he heard Junior say, "You know I didn't come down here to see Blackstone. Are you frigid? How in the world did Larry live with you? You are a cold bitch."

When Dale was near, he could see a LED lantern on the ground that glowed behind Katherine and Junior. He was about to speak when he heard a slap, and Katherine said, "Junior Maddox, you are a cruel man."

In an instant, he heard Junior slap Katherine with a great force as he said, "I'll take you right here, bitch."

Dale ran the rest of the way and leaped towards Junior Maddox. Both men hit the ground. Katherine was stunned and just stood watching Dale and Junior hitting each other as they rolled on the ground.

Junior yelled, "Katherine, call 911. This fool is trying to kill me." When Katherine heard him yell to call 911, she started crying and laughing at the same time.

When both men stood, He grabbed Junior and pinned Junior's neck in the crook of his arm. At the same time, Dale pulled Junior's left arm to his back. Junior could not move. Dale held him until Junior passed out.

Katherine saw Junior go limp. She yelled to Dale, "Don't kill him, Dale. He's not worth it."

Dale stood up and walked over to Katherine. She fell into his arms and started crying again. Dale held her without saying a word as he stroked her hair until all the sobs stopped.

Katherine pulled back a little from Dale as she looked at Junior on the ground. Her voice trembled as she said, "Is he dead?"

Dale dropped his arms away from Katherine, picked up the lantern, and went over to Junior. He looked at Katherine and smiled, "Nope. He's just passed out for a while. He will be fine. Do you want to kick him, Katherine? He'll never know it, but it might make you feel better."

Katherine started laughing and said, "I hate to kick a good man while he is down. Oh...but he is not a good man." She walked over to Junior and shoved her foot against his ribs.

She looked at Dale, and her smile grew. She pulled her leg back and kicked Junior in the ribs as hard as she could. Junior grunted, and Katherine looked upward and said, "God forgive me. I know vengeance is not mine. But God, it made me feel much better. Junior made me feel dirty, but now I don't feel dirty anymore. Thank you for listening, God."

Dale looked at Katherine with all the love any man could have for a woman. He quickly turned away because he didn't want her to see how much he cared for her.

He knew if he had to, he would have killed Junior to protect her. He was thankful he didn't have to go that far, but Dale knew he had made a dangerous enemy.

As Junior was waking up, Dale shined the flashlight on him. When he got up from the ground, he grabbed his right side.

Katherine snickered, and Dale reached over and rubbed the top of her head like he had seen E.H. rub Skylar's head. He guessed it must be a sign of affection.

Junior walked up to them and stopped, "You two better watch your back. You messed with the wrong man."

As Junior walks up the incline to the Denton's yard, Dale and Katherine followed about twenty feet behind him. Nobody spoke until Junior got into his truck and left.

Katherine then kissed Dale on the cheek and said, "I think we should not tell E.H. about this. He's a godly man, but I am not sure how he would handle this."

Dale smiled and said, "Tell E. H. about what?" but he was also thinking how near Brutus was to be locked up for a very long time and soon.

EPISODE 65

When E. H. mentioned going to the North Carolina State Fairgrounds for the 4th of July celebration, Katherine barely held back the tears. All she could think about was Larry had to work the year before.

She, E. H., Dale, Pam, Stanley, Martin, and Dorothy had been there, but she had missed Larry. There had been a lot of laughter and camaraderie, which helped her to cope.

However, this year Larry and Pam were gone, and Stanley and Dale had something else to do. This year her 4th of July" would be celebrated with Jordan, Skylar, and E. H.

A couple of days later, after the children had gone to bed, E. H. presented her with another option. He said, "I understand why you do not want to go to Raleigh for the fireworks. I was at the Webb's Mill fishing the other day, and a man from Southport came and began talking about the Southport 4th of July festival there."

"It sounded nice, so I asked him about somewhere to stay. He said most motels booked, but he and his wife have a barn behind their house. They turned into a small vacation rental. He said they had not rented it this year but would be glad for us to use it."

"What kind of celebration?" Katherine asked.

E. H. pulled out his billfold and took a paper out, and handed it to Katherine as he said, "Here is the address of the site of the festival activities."

Halfheartedly, Katherine pulled up the web page. "She began to read aloud some of the events, "A patriotic parade, arts and crafts, a naturalization ceremony, car show, military band, other music events, concessions, face painting, sack races and river activities." She abruptly stopped, cleared her throat, and continued...and, firefighter's competition."

E. H. said, "I'm sorry."

She smiled and said, "You don't have to be sorry. I think all this sounds good. It's on the river also. I believe it might be what we need. If you are sure the gentleman you talked with will let us stay at the barn, go ahead and plan for the three-day stay. Would there be room for Martin and Dorothy?"

E. H. said, "Martin said he and Dorothy were flying to Georgia to see their grandchildren so that it would be just the four of us. What do you think?"

"I think we need to go, E. H. As soon as you find out about the room, you can tell the children," said Katherine.

EPISODE 66

Dale, Stanley, and four other men stood in a line listening to one of Junior Maddox's minions. He was barking the same orders Dale and Stanley listened to before the Ides of March party.

The minion dressed as if he were a military officer and stood with his chest puffed out. Stanley was concentrating more on not laughing at the Maddox stooge than he was on the instructions.

Dale listened to the instructions on how to park cars as intently as possible, but he could not help to be amused. On the way over to the Stonehouse Farm, he and Stanley had talked about the previous party.

Stanley had called The-Man, a little tin soldier: the little Napoleon. Both he and Stanley had a good laugh, and it relieved some of the tension, but both men knew the night could become deadly for them and others if all didn't go perfect.

While the Little Ten Soldier was baying at the six valets in the parking lot, Junior Maddox was in his office shouting at the humble Cotton. "What do you expect me to do? Our product doesn't come with instructions.

If the junkies want to chase the dragon and knock themselves off, it is not our problem. The China White is selling faster than we can get it.

The shipment tonight will be three times our usual order. And, I should not have to remind you of your cut of this shipment. It will make you an exceedingly rich man."

Cotton stood attentive as usual. It was the first time he mentioned any doubt about the product they brought in. Cotton didn't do the hard drugs, but he occasionally smoked pot, and he was a silent millionaire because of his work with Maddox.

However, he lost a Viet Nam buddy three days earlier. Cotton didn't sell drugs, but he felt culpable in his longtime friend's death. He helped put the drugs on the streets of Stonehope and other Blackstone County towns.

Junior added, "Can you do your job tonight?" but Junior was thinking, damn, he is going to be hard to replace.

Before Cotton turned, he said, "Yes, Sir. You can count on me as always." He made his words sound sincere, but he saw the expression on Junior Maddox's face. He had seen it before, and people disappeared after receiving the death glare.

As Cotton turned, Junior added, "Cotton, how is your family doing?"

Cotton continued walking and did not turn around. He knew he had to make a lifesaving decision for him and his family before the night was up.

However, he had no idea the night would ultimately end Junior Maddox's drug business and how many people would die.

EPISODE 67

Less than five miles away in a wooded farm path where the tree canopy was so thick not even a helicopter could detect the 18-wheeler loaded with toilet tissue and Junior Maddox's drugs. It

The load was being removed and put into three different limousines. In each limousine was a passenger; each a lieutenant of Junior's illegal business. Several undocumented Hispanic men completed the unloading and transferring of the drugs—they who had no idea each were tagged as expendable.

The undocumented men unloading the truck and waiting for the van to take them to another state where they were guaranteed work. They could see the van and were laughing and talking about their stroke of luck.

The workers had no idea when they neared their destination; the back of a van would slowly fill with laughing gas and, later, Fluothane.

Then, the workers, driven into a watery grave, and all but the driver would drown. It was not The-Man's first time ridding Junior Maddox of witnesses. To him, it was only a way of making more money than an uneducated man could ever dream.

The driver of the 18-wheeler had no idea the undocumented men used to unload would be killed. He was grateful for his excellent paying job, driving the same truck around with various loads; sometimes, the load included drugs, sometimes not.

Junior always felt superior after each multimillion-dollar load went into his barns. He knew he had perfected a system. No one could discover his brilliant building nor his drugs.

Operatives circled drones above the Stonehouse farm compound as they had in three previous drug deliveries and **one** drug run leaving the farm.

They realized heat signatures from the tunnels were weak on those attempts but could detect live bodies. The signals from the underground garages, on this as with other delivery dates, were strong.

One of the men Junior had invited had to say he couldn't come. He faked a back injury that had put him in a wheelchair. Junior explained to him they had access to wheelchairs and asked him to please come anyway.

Unbeknown to Junior, his influential friend, and attorney was an undercover DEA operative. The panel van which delivered the man who used a wheelchair was also the van tricked out with all the most recent electronic equipment needed for Junior's takedown.

And, it was parked right in the guest parking lot with four technological geniuses inside. Not only were they smart, but battle-tested and ready if needed.

Junior Maddox's sociopathic personality made him believe his way was the best, and it all worked because it was supposed to. He charmed others with his charisma and stories.

He exaggerated his abilities, his accomplishments, his travels, and his friendships with famous people. He was a master wordsmith and sometimes actually believed his own stories.

Junior was self-serving and could simulate love or compassion to get what he wanted. Junior believed his charisma and intelligence made him indestructible

As far as Junior was concerned, his setup at the Stonehouse farm was perfect, so he saw no need to be careful. It had been working for years.

This belief, combined with his lack of shame, guilt, or remorse, allowed him to betray, threaten, harm people, or kill them to reach his intended goal.

EPISODE 68

Maddox's three limousines came in staggered between other vehicles coming to the 4th of July party. The driver of the first limousine rolled down his window and spoke to Stanley. He used the code word preset for the take-down mission as he told Stanley there were two more limousines on the way with the product.

He said, "you can recognize them by the first three characters on their license plates; JM1."

Stanley thought *Junior Maddox would help the takedown by his arrogance.*

Each limo drove by the guest-parking area and towards the stables. Each turned onto the grass and then the concrete pad behind the stables. As a large door opened, they drove in, and the lieutenants got out helped unload their goods.

Once unloaded onto heavy-duty rolling carts, the driver drove out of the hidden garage area and back to the guest parking lot. Each lieutenant stayed to make sure the workers adequately stacked his load in the tack house.

Cotton made sure each lieutenant was gone before he pressed a button hidden in the office desk. The wall of saddles, bridles, and other tack rolled open to unload the drugs to the elevator platform.

Once all three loads lay on carts in the tack house, Cotton used the elevator controls to take each load down to the tunnel. There he would roll the drugs into Barn A and neatly stack them on shelving waiting for delivery around the east coast.

Junior's grand party was to begin at eight o'clock. Junior picked up the intercom and addressed his one hundred-eighty guest, saying, "Have a good time, drink-up, partake in the chefs' creations, be merry, and fireworks are to begin at ten o'clock."

When Junior's voice left the sound system, county music filled all areas of the event, which included the main house, the barbeque shelter, and the pool area.

The air was still, and thunder rumbled in the distance. The break-in vehicle arrivals gave Dale a chance to speak to Stanley. Scarcely auditable, he said, "I went into the van and found we are in the path of a large thunderstorm with considerable lightning and heavy downpours. It is estimated to be about fifteen minutes from here."

As if on cue, Junior's voice reverberated across the Stonehouse Farm estate, "Guest, there is a storm headed our way. Please take shelter in the pool house, the enclosed portion of the barbeque shelter, or the main house.

According to the weather report, this storm will come with strong winds and lightning. The best part is it will be out of our area in time for the fireworks. Please keep eating and drinking while we have some of mother nature's 4th of July celebration."

Thinking about how clever he sounded, Junior downed his shot of bourbon and walked towards Sunny Tupelo, who is entertaining her admiring fans.

She was standing only three feet from the library door. As she was talking, she kept an eye on Junior. Her job was to let the undercover assets know when Junior left the main house or entered the library.

She threw her head back and laughed at some comment one of the guests made as Junior Maddox put a large, old key into the library lock. She watched him go in, close the door, and she heard the door lock from the inside. The trip to the library was earlier than predicted. She had to think fast.

The intercom station was only a few feet away. As the lightning, the thunder, and the pouring rain surrounded the estate, Sunny walked over and picked up the microphone and said, "This is for Mother Nature."

She began singing The Star-Spangled Banner a cappella, *"Oh, say can you see by the dawn's early light. What so proudly we hailed at the twilight's last gleaming."*

Sunny Tupelo's first song was the signal to begin the take-down. As the song sounded on the speakers, the strong wind began. Stanley and Dale ran to the shelter surrounding the front of the horse Stables.

As they stood there, Cotton ran up and said, "I have to go in and calm the horses." Getting into the stables was just what Dale and Stanley wanted to do.

Dale and Stanley knew Martin Webb was supposed to slip away from the cooking of barbeque and hide in the tack-room of the horse stables. The timing was off, but they looked at each other and shrugged. Dale said to Cotton, "Must be a lot of horses in there. We'll go in and help."

Thunder boomed, and it sounded as if the lightning had struck just feet away. Cotton opened the stable door and ran to the opposite end of the stables. For a few moments, he forgot about his duties of opening the tunnel door.

The metal roof of the stables intensified the thunder and the storm's pounding rain. Cotton, more concerned about the horses, began loudly whistling a calming tune. Dale and Stanley joined in.

The horses started to calm as the thunder moved further and further away. Suddenly Cotton remembered what he was supposed to be doing.

He had already made one mistake by questioning Junior Maddox, and now he was late opening his side of the door between the two barns. Cotton's two-way radio had constantly beeped while trying to calm the horses.

Cotton panicked and ran to the tack room door and unlocked it before remembering two other men in the stables. He quickly entered the room with Dale and Stanley right behind him. However, someone inside grabbed his arm, pulled him into a choke-hold, and put a hand over his mouth.

At first, Cotton believed it was Junior, but then he saw the face of Martin Webb. He knew they were a part of the FBI raid but was still frightened they also might be on Maddox's side. His life and the life of his family depended on how all this went down.

EPISODE 69

After Junior closed the secret library door, he followed the tunnel to and through Barn B's basement. He stood at the tunnel's steel door, halfway between Barn A and Barn B. The door separated him from a half-billion-dollar drug shipment.

He took a deep breath and pumped his chest out. He considered all the time and energy it had taken to build his drug empire and how it was impenetrable. He knew it was earlier than he had planned, but he was confident everything would be as always.

The load he was housing tonight would be the largest and the most profitable ever. He could hardly wait for the millions to roll in. However, there were a couple of problems he had to solve. Cotton and his family would be first. Then, he would choose someone else to take Cotton's place.

Junior Maddox knew the crew who unloaded the eighteen-wheeler were on their last journey. As in his past shipments, he smiled to himself and thought, *it is always better to rid yourself of loose lips before they can harm you*.

There will always be undocumented workers who want to make big bucks, and no one ever misses them after they are gone. Junior knew only one van load of workers discovered in their watery grave, but there was no way it could ever connect to his empire.

He smiled, took out his walkie-talkie, and again hit the button for Cotton to answer. He then deactivated the lock on his side of the metal door by putting his right eye close to the iris scanner.

Junior called for Cotton two more times. He wasn't upset since he knew the plan was ahead of schedule. However, after the fifth time, Cotton did not answer Junior was livid.

As minutes passed, he became enraged. When he heard Cotton's voice, he snapped at him. As the locked door began to open, Junior wished he had a firearm to end Cotton. He had no idea his world was crashing.

If at that point, someone had told Junior what had happened while he was waiting for Cotton, he would have assumed it was a joke.

Martin had a key during the wait and slipped into the tack room while Cotton, Stanley, and Dale were trying to calm the horses.

Martin also knew the horse feed, delivered earlier in the day, contained guns and ammo. He had already opened the horse feed bags and removed the shrink-wrapped protected firearms and ammunition; 3 Springfield 1911 .45 pistols with loaded rounds and extra loaded clips.

Cotton had not been surprised when Dale, Martin, and Stanley came into the tack room, but when he saw the guns laying on the unopened feed bags, his eyes had widened, and his countenance had sagged. Cotton had known his only chance was if the plan went as it was supposed to.

As Dale, Stanley, and Martin placed the pistols in their back-waist band and put the extra clips in their pants pocket Martin had said, "If I let you go, don't make a loud noise, or you are a dead man. I'll snap your neck right here."

Cotton had bobbed his head up and down, desperate to speak. When Martin took his hand away, Cotton softly said, "I am still on your side, so don't kill me. I will help you in any way you want.

He's going to kill my family and me tonight, so you are the only hope I have. Please, don't kill me."

Who is going to kill you? Martin had asked.

"Junior Maddox and his lieutenants," Cotton had said as his two-way radio blasted with Junior's voice.

"Cotton, you are a dead man if you don't answer," yelled Junior.

Terrified, Cotton said, "If I don't answer now, he will send someone after me, and my whole family will be dead within the hour."

Martin quickly told Cotton, "We know you are the only one who can open this side of the door between here and the library tunnel."

Martin forgetting his earbuds were operational as soon as Sunny Tupelo began singing, forgot his words were going directly to the panel van. Martin looked at Dale and said, "Radio Inrun59 and tell her to send a rescue unit to Cotton's house.

Martin told Cotton," If you want to see your family again, talk to Junior and sound like you usually do."

Cotton answered, "I'm coming, Boss."

All four men had descended to Tunnel A. When they were just a few feet in, Martin grabbed the back of Cotton's collar and had whispered, "How many men will be on the other side of the door with Junior, and are they armed?"

"It will only be Junior, and he is never armed." Cotton whispered.

Stanley had spoken with malice in his voice, "If you are wrong, Junior won't have time to kill you. I'll do it myself."

Martin had let go of Cotton's collar. Cotton continued to the locked door, and once there, he placed his eye near the iris reader and then stepped back.

EPISODE 70

When the door finally opened, Junior Maddox froze. His mind could not comprehend why Martin Webb, Stanley Hall, and Dale Weaver were there.

In an instant, he began fabricating his story saying, "Thank God, you are here. I went to the library, and something hit my head. When I regained consciousness, I was lying in this tunnel. Do you know where we are?"

All four men were taken aback by the sincere and almost believable performance, but Dale quickly grabbed Junior, pushed him towards the other men, and said, "Walk." They backtracked to the basement of Barn A, where the new drugs sat neatly stacked.

When Junior saw the stacks of drugs, he saw millions of dollars, but he cried out, "What in the hell is this? Where are we? Are these drugs? Are Y'all drug dealers? Cotton, *what* have *you* been doing?"

At the same time, he was pretending to be dumbfounded. He kept keying his radio with 666. To his guards, it meant something had gone wrong.

Above ground, his Hench-men were looking around for the problem. Previously, there had never been any situations where anything went wrong while at the Stonehouse Farm. They began leaving their stations and running to other stations to ask if anyone knew what was going on.

Still perplexed, the guards formed a circle behind the pond area and began yelling at each other. None of them knew about the tunnels or the drug storage under the barns.

The lightning and rain were over, and Junior's guards began accusing and yelling at each other as if they were in an episode of The Stooges.

Some of the guests heard the commotion and began to make their circle around the guards. They thought it was some type of entertainment their host planned.

When they began clapping, the men became quiet. They looked around, thinking the guests were right about them being the entertainment. They held their weapons up and pointed them into the air, and began shooting.

The crowd clapped louder. Then several DEA agents ran towards the commotion and yelled for the people to go inside. One DEA agent ran into the stables as the audience outside clapped and whistled, thinking it was still an act.

In a blink of an eye, the guards began shooting their machine guns and pistols towards the agents. People started falling, running, and screaming. The agents had no choice but to shoot the guards who still huddled in a group.

The technicians saw the movement of the guards by their heat signature. They had also watched as some of the party-goers had surrounded them.

The short series of events was a perfect storm. It had happened so quickly, and the outcome was not predictable. The technicians in the van called the county for multiple ambulances.

Moments after the gunshots ended, Martin, Cotton, Dale, Stanley, and Junior stepped out of the tack house. Junior was cuffed and held at gunpoint. Junior continued to swear he was innocent. He said over and over, "I am the victim."

The agent who had run into the horse stables told Martin, Dale, Cotton, and Stanley to wait fifteen minutes before coming out of the stables and going out the back door. He grabbed Junior and roughly pushed him towards the stable door.

When the shooting stopped, Martin, Cotton, Dale, and Stanley exited the rear of the horse barn just in time to hear Junior yelling how the agents were to blame for the people who lay wounded and dead on the ground.

Handcuffed, Junior lead forward. He saw a dark figure of a person sauntering towards the woods. Junior grits his teeth with hatred.

The person he knew as The-Man was slipping into the woods as if he were taking a simple afternoon stroll. Junior's fear of the man's barbarism checked his need to point out The-Man to his captors.

He thought *I'll get out of this, and then I will hunt him down. He will be sorry he was ever born.*

The agent was still holding his catch. It made Junior became louder and more adamant about his innocence; one of his stable boys stepped out of the shadows, walked towards Junior, pulled a gun from the back-waist of his pants, and shot Junior Maddox once in the heart.

Immediately he threw his gun down, held his hands in the air, and dropped to his knees, and in broken English, he said, "Junior Maddox is a bad man. He killed my brother and two of my cousins because they were undocumented." He said no more as they cuffed him.

When Dale, Stanley, and Martin gathered in front of the barn, they were confused. But each walked to their positions as valets and bartenders. Later they would find Martin, Cooksey, and Rodney had arrested three hierarchies of a Columbia cartel inside the house.

Two days later, Vernon Maddox mourned at the grave of his son. There had not been a funeral, but E. H. Denton had come to pray over the coffin before being lowered.

Afterward, Vernon thanked E. H. and said, "You are probably the only person around who knows what I am going through. No matter what Junior did, he was still my son."

E. H. shook Vernon's hand to acknowledge he did know how Vernon felt. One week later, Vernon's retirement began.

He sold his house and all his belonging except a few clothes. He purchased a luxurious RV with space for Pearl and their daughter, Vernel.

He drove to Baltimore, he and Pearl were married, and they began their adventure by taking Vernel to Disney World and out west to the Grand Canyon.

EPISODE 71

Dale laid his phone on the kitchen table. He walked over to the window and looked out. There was not a cloud in the sky, and the TV weather reporter had said it would be a copy of the day before. He had planned to work in the garage, but E. H. Denton had called and wanted Dale to have breakfast with him and go for a walk on the farm. Dale went down the stairs and saw his boss was already at work on the 56 Ford. A frequent customer brought it in the day before. He said, "Morning, Rodney. How's it looking?"

Rodney reached for a notepad and wrote something on it while saying, "Everything under the hood may need replacing. I'm making a list now."

"Hope the owner has deep pockets."

"Yeah, he does. Very deep," he said as he laid the pad on the fender. "Are you working in those clothes?"

"No, E. H. Denton called and wants me to come out and spends some time with him."

Rodney said, "He's a good man. It's going to be a nice day, so if I don't see you this afternoon, I'll see you tomorrow."

"Yeah, see you," and motioned for Mozart to get into the truck.

As Dale was riding out to the Denton place, he wondered why E. H. would call him to come out on a weekday. When he turned onto the driveway, he noticed E. H.'s truck was the only vehicle there.

He stopped, got out of his truck, let Mozart out, went up the back porch steps, opened the screened door, and started to knock on the back door. Before he could, E. H. opened the door. The smell of the country ham and fresh biscuits filled the room.

"Glad you could come, Dale." E. H. said as he gave Dale a bear hug."

Dale had grown accustomed to the way E. H. greeted him and returned the hug.

E. H. said, "Have a seat," as he pointed to the chair at the end of the table. He opened the oven door and took out a large pan of homemade biscuits. He put the pan onto the counter and carefully began to put the biscuit into a basket lined with a linen napkin.

"Who else is coming?" asked Dale.

E. H looked at him with his brow arching as he realized why Dale asked the question. E. H. had cooked a lot of food. "Just us," He said with a chuckle.

He put the basket of biscuits on the table, walked to the refrigerator and retrieved peach preserves, put the jar on the table, pulled out the chair adjacent to Dale, and said, "I made you hash browns because I know you are not fond of grits."

"E. H., I will not need to eat anything the rest of the day. You made a breakfast feast," said Dale with a laugh.

E. H. reached over and put his hand over Dale's and began the blessing. When finished, he said, "Let's eat."

As they ate, Dale and E. H. talked about some of the things going on in Dale's life. E. H. also talked about the Denton family. When they finished breakfast, Dale helped E. H. clear the table and put the remaining food away.

It seemed to Dale, E. H. was becoming tense, so he asked, "Is there something wrong, E. H.? You look worried."

"Let's walk, Dale. I will tell you what is on my mind."

As the two men went out the back door, Ratchet and Mozart run from under the porch. The dogs had made friends with each other not long after Dale took him from the diner.

When Dale and E. H. walked towards the path, they had seen E. H. take many times they ran ahead of the two men.

Ratchet and Mozart knew they were going towards the enormous boulders called Blackstone. The men were quiet as they watched Mozart come back for the old Ratchet over and over.

When they all arrived at the boulders, the two men and the two dogs stood looking in the field beyond Blackstone.

Dale stayed quiet as he looked at E. H. now and then. He was waiting for him to speak. In a few minutes, E. H. said, "let's continue walking along the path by the wooded area."

They walked about a half-mile until they arrived at a circular spot that was bare of any vegetation. It was twenty-five feet in diameter. The dogs stood outside the circle and would not go in.

He turned to Dale and said, "Son, I was standing beside the boulders the night you came. I saw you leave the craft. I saw you walk a few feet away, and then the craft ascended vertically and disappeared."

Dale was speechless as E. H. continued. "I've seen the craft land here several times, as my father has, and his father before him.

It has been a secret of the Denton men since our ancestors obtained this land. A Native American medicine man passed on the first knowledge."

"Did Larry know about the landings?" Dale asked.

"He learned on this twenty-first birthday as all the Denton men were, but he did not know you arrived on the craft."

"Does Martin know?"

"No. *He* is not a Denton. I've wished many times I could tell him.

"I did not know there had been other landings. No one told me," said Dale.

"You were not the first I saw to leave the craft and stay close. The others took a path northwards and followed the railroad tracts toward the town of Stonehope. I do not know if you were the only one who stayed in Stonehope."

"Are you aware of anyone else who has seen the circle where nothing grows?" Dale asked."

"Yes, many people have seen the spot, but they hear another story which the Native Americans also passed on. They called it a circle of the gods, and each full moon, the medicine men, would place food, water, and weapons within the circle."

However, they did not tell anyone but my Great-great Grandfather about the items left by the natives being taking by the craft and leaving metal weapons and farming tools in their place

Dale walked to the center of the circle, bent down, and picked up some sandy soil; he smelled the earth. He looked at E. H. and said, "There are no animal tracks inside the circle."

E. H. said, "I know. The animals will not walk anywhere in the circle, and the birds will not fly near it or over it."

Dale walked back towards E. H. and asked, "Why did you bring me out here, E. H.?"

"I have some questions." E. H. said,

Dale said, "Let's walk back towards Blackstone, and I will answer the questions if I can."

As they walked, E. H. asked, "I have been searching the internet while looking at the names of galaxies discovered by humans.

Where are you from, and why are you here? Does our government know about you or the others who have come to help us?"

"I am from a galaxy near the Milky Way, and I, as well as others, come to help erase the plagues on the earth."

Both men stopped and faced each other, and Dale began talking again.

"E. H. I'm going to tell you things I shouldn't. I believe you are an honest and honorable man. You cannot tell anyone else. It could be very dangerous for you and your family. Do you still want to know?"

E. H. nodded his head, and the two men began walking as Dale continued, "I assume you know about the Roswell, New Mexico incident of 1946 where it was reported a spaceship crashed."

He saw E. H. nod again, and Dale said, "Soon after the report in newspapers, the government gave another statement saying it was a weather balloon.

A spaceship did crash near Roswell. The military removed the spacecraft and three bodies. All the evidence was removed and shipped to a small aircraft hangar in Area 51 in Nevada."

"In 1956, the military began to use Area 51 for flight testing. The site now covers a rectangular area measuring twenty-three by twenty-five miles, and it has seven undergrown floors. It is the central point for extra-terrestrial communications."

E. H. interrupted, "Why, after all these years hasn't the U. S. Government told the truth?"

Dale said, "I can only tell you what I know while I was on my planet. All the cadets' orders said the people would panic if they knew there were extra-terrestrials on earth. Have you ever heard about Valiant Thor?"

"Is he the one some conspiracy theorists say came to earth to help and met the president?" E. H. asked.

"Yes. Valiant Thor was, but the name was given to him by government officials. They felt that if anyone found out about the meetings, the name would be enough to make the incident like many others; laughable and unbelievable."

"However, many lies came from the visit up during and after his visit. Therefore, people believe it was a hoax. The basis of the Val visit was to let the world know there was a group of nine planets which formed an assembly to aid Earth."

Dale continues, "The space traveler, Val, proclaimed he came to let the people of Earth know of many interstellar concerns. He did talk to the president of the time and asked to speak to other Earth leaders. No one would listen."

"Are you saying there was no Jesus and this Val Thor is the one who visited earth?" E. H. blurted out.

"No, E. H., not at all. Jesus was and is real and historical writings are true to the word." Dale continued to explain, "I am trying to tell you the United States and all other countries know aliens, as they call them, are here on Earth and have been for thousands of years. It's in many ancient documents."

"Some help as I am trying to do and some in other ways. However, there is only so much we can do.

Part of our promise before we come to earth states, we must allow mistakes to happen no matter how terrible. Only God has the wisdom and the right to change anyone or anything on earth, and since He can see the future, it is hard for humans as well as aliens to understand why bad things happen."

The two men stopped and looked into each other's eyes without speaking. A few minutes passed, and E. H. said, "I still don't understand why governments do not tell us what is going on. I believe we are smart enough to cope."

Dale put both hands on E. H.'s shoulders and said, "Some will but some will not. The fact is that countries are easing humans into accepting a lot of things they do not understand by creating TV shows and movies where humans and extra-terrestrials try to get along with each other."

"You mean like Star Trek?" Asked E. H.

"Yes, like Star Trek. Do you remember one of the first aliens on TV?" asked Dale. "It was Mork, the NANU guy,"

E. H. chuckled and said, "How about ALF?"

Dale also laughed and said, "Yes, him too. Do you see where I am going? Sometimes it takes a long time to prepare humans for significant changes. The earth still has problems with people who do not look like them.

People distrust someone who comes into their community with different looks, a foreign language, different clothing, different colored skin, or different music. They sometimes don't trust them or worse; they don't believe the other looking people are as intelligent as they are."

"Can you imagine how some humans would feel if extra-terrestrials aliens moved next to them? Even aliens who looked human would cause major problems. And, if they didn't look human most people would be terrified; not just in the United States but in other countries too," Dale said.

E. H. said, "Dale, I see your point. Can we go to my house and talk more about this? I need a cup of coffee."

Dale and E. H. fell in step with one another with the dogs behind them. They arrived, and once inside, E. H. made coffee. Dale asked for a Dr. Pepper as E. H. took a platter of crisp apple muffins from the cabinet and put it on the table.

Once they had eaten muffins and had a liquid refreshment, E. H. said, "I must confess the aircraft landing on the farm has bothered me for a long time but what you just told me bothers me more. I know you said God is in control of these things, but why don't I see them in the Bible?"

Dale was shaking his head as he said, "E. H., the last thing I wanted to do was upset you.

"I know, Dale. However, scientists on earth are talking about the God particle and the Big Bang Theory. I can't see how all this fits." E. H. said.

Dale asked, "Do you remember I said a few minutes ago we weren't given the wisdom to interfere with how planet earth is evolving?"

"Yes, I remember," E. H. said.

"I do not know the timetable of God, and neither does anyone else. I asked questions when I became a cadet so let me try to explain."

"Scientists on earth make discoveries all the time, and they sometimes act as if it is the final answer. The God particle is far from being the final answer. In God's time, Earth is still an embryo." Dale said.

E. H. asked, "What about the Big Bang Theory?"

"The Big Bang is a theory, and Earth scientists are still evolving," Dale said.

Sheepishly E. H. gazed at Dale and then said, "I was going to ask you why you were here."

"I am here to help with the plague of drug trafficking. I was on earth five years before I came to this area."

"How can one man help with drug trafficking?" asked E. H.

"There are many of us. We are all over the world trying to stop drug trafficking. Others are here to help in other areas such as war, greed, men with too much power, and also with human diseases and ailments."

E. H. scratched the back of his neck and said, "Your people have been coming a long time, but it appears the earth is getting worse, not better."

Dale put his Dr. Pepper down and said, "I know it looks that way. God uses us to do His will, so if we had not been here all these thousands of years, your Earth would be as Mars."

E. H. looked at Dale as if he were his son and said, "Thank you for taking the time to explain. I have so many more questions," and immediately, E. H. asked, "Why did Larry have to die?"

Dale said, "I do not know the answer."

E. H. looked at his coffee cup and asked, "Are you a human?"

"I think you know the answer, E. H."

"Again, E. H. had a question, "When you were lying hurt by the road the night we found you; I wondered if my sister and Martin were your earth parents. Are they?"

"Why do you ask?" Dale said.

"Years ago, Dorothy and Martin told me they were abducted to a flying saucer and had things done to them. They believed the beings took sperm from Martin and eggs from Dorothy."

"I found it hard to believe something like that could happen. I thought maybe each had some nightmare, but I still was puzzled why both had the same nightmare."

E. H. continued, "Even after Martin told me what had happened, I found it hard to believe until Dorothy showed me the scar on her belly. Martin said he had a scar on his groin, and I knew he wouldn't lie."

"Still, I found it hard to believe. I know my sister is a Christian and would never make up a story for any reason."

E. H. hesitated and then said, "The first night I saw you, I thought you looked like Stephen, Dorothy's son. The day you came to Webb's Mill when we were fishing, I pretended I had not noticed the resemblance, but I did notice it."

"On the night we found you, the story Dorothy and Martin told years before came flooding into my mind." E. H. hesitated again, "So we are related?" He said as he smiled at Dale.

Dale shifted from his position and said, "I did not receive my parents' names, but I do know my planet does harvest human eggs, sperm, and DNA of Earth people."

"Since I look so much like Stephen, I believe I am from Martin's and Dorothy's extractions. I do not believe it would be a good idea for them to know. I will be leaving soon."

"You can't," said E. H. "You are in love with Katherine. You can't leave."

"E. H., it is not my decision. My seven-year tour will be over soon. I don't have a choice, and I am not in love with Katherine."

"We can talk about who loves whom later. Right now, I want to know why you can't stay. You can still work to make this Earth a better place."

I believe you would be more than suitable for Katherine. Can you do something to stay? Can I do something so you can stay?"

" We need you," E. H. pleaded and rose from his sitting position while yelling at Dale. "What can I do? I love you like my own son. Who can I talk to?"

Dale stood and griped E. H.'s arms. "E. H., calm down. Please calm down." He kept repeating the word until E. H. was quiet, and then he said, "E. H. the cadets who come to Earth do not have a choice. They are not supposed to get involved with other humans. I have made a huge mistake, and now I care about people, and they care about me. I never wanted to hurt you or anyone else. I'm sorry. I have to go. If I stay, I will die."

E. H. became calm, and Dale dropped his hands to his side and said, "I'm sorry."

Dale watched as E. H. sat back down, looking defeated. E. H turned, looked at Dale, and said, "Son, we have a lot to do. I cannot let you go. I can still pray. He will hear me." E. H. hesitated and asked, "You are sure God is real?"

Without hesitation, Dale said, "Absolutely. There is a God of the Universe. Don't stop believing. He does hear you, but you already know He hears you."

EPISODE 72

It was August third and only a few minutes before midnight. It would be his birthday one second after both clock hands reached twelve. It also meant Dale's seven-year tour of duty was over. He had to leave.

Dale had spent each day since Brutus's takedown visiting his friends. In July, the third Saturday, E. H. had thrown him an early birthday party in the church social room.

Everyone Dale knew in Blackstone County had been invited. Only he and E. H. knew it was also a going-away party. Somehow, Stanley had convinced Sunny Tupelo to come and be part of the celebration. Vernon, Pearl, and Vernel had left their Wyoming home to attend the party.

Dale had explained to E. H. he would not die when he went back to his planet. He told E. H. if he ever saw him again, he would be a different person.

The process of brain mapping would begin as soon as he was on the transport back to his planet. He would not remember anyone, a place, or any time.

Dale said, "I will be re-programed as if I were a robot. All memories of being on earth would be gone. I will be given another name and can be sent anywhere in the universe."

As Dale finished telling E. H. what would happen, tears running down his cheeks, and sobs racked his body. E. H.

stepped forward and put his arms around Dale until he stopped crying. E. H. felt like doing the same thing, but he wanted to be strong for his nephew.

Dale could have never imagined the way people treated him the night of the party. Even though it would be painful, he wanted to keep all the memories, the good ones, and the bad ones. His biggest regret was not finding Dwight Gacy and making him pay for Pam's death.

Dale had E. H. for no one to get him a gift. However, E. H. and several others had commissioned Rodney to carve a three-foot image of Dale. After the meal and a giant birthday cake shaped and colored like his 1957 Bel Air. Then E. H. brought out the huge gift-wrapped present.

After Dale unwrapped, the present everyone began to laugh. The carved image was of Dale wearing a cowboy hat and holding a lassoed sphere.

When Dale saw the carved figure, he immediately wondered if E. H. told people about his interstellar travels. When Dale looked at him, E. H. held his hands out palms up and shrugged his shoulders, and mouthed, "I didn't know."

Dale started to laugh too, but he also wanted to cry. He had made individual visits to Martin and Dorothy Webb. They showed pictures of Stephen, who Dale knew was his brother, his family. He never mentions he was their son.

He and Stanley had been back to Minnesott Beach and did some inlet fishing. He took Katherine, Jordan, and Skylar on a camping trip near Boone, North Carolina. He also had spent a lot of time talking with E. H.

Dale sat until it became light outside, and then he showered, shaved, dressed, and headed to the cemetery to visit with Pam. He told her about the drug cartel takedown and thanked her for all the laughs. He said, "Ok. I am the one talking the most today, but I love you, Sis."

He stopped by Edward's Diner and had breakfast. He talked to Cooksey for a few minutes and then headed to E. H.'s home. When he knocked on the back door, Katherine came to the door. Dale's heart seemed to stop when he saw her sleepy face.

When he went into the house, he saw Jordan and Skylar sitting at the table eating cereal. Their smiles uplifted his spirits, but just as fast, it was gone. He was struggling with how to say goodbye to people who didn't know he was leaving.

The children saw packages under his arm, and Jordan asked about them. Dale said, "When you finish eating your breakfast, we will open them." Both children began eating as fast as they could as Katherine and Dale laughed.

Katherine told her children to put their dishes in the dishwasher and then sit back down when they finished. Quickly they did as they were asked and then sat looking at Dale as if they were puppies waiting for dog biscuits.

Dale handed a package to each. Jordan opened his first and said, "Wow, a LEGO kit of the Yoda's Jedi Starfighter and a lightsaber.

Before Jordan could say anything more, Skylar squealed, "A Princess Leia Doll and a Princess Leia LEGO fashion set."

Katherine looked inquisitively at Dale. He threw his head back and laughed before saying, "Don't be mad, Mom. I just wanted to give them something special."

Before Katherine could say anything, else E. H. walked in. Both Jordan and Skylar were trying to get the attention of their grandfather. E. H. held his hand up, and both kids became quiet.

E. H. looked at the gifts and then looked at Dale; he understood the reference. However, he played perplexed as he asked, "Did I miss someone's birthday?"

In unison, the children yelled, "No." E. H. turned to Dale and said, "This was nice of you, Dale. What are we celebrating?" Even though E. H. knew Dale would be leaving soon after dark; he could not tell the news to his family.

Dale looked at his friend and said, "We are celebrating Jordan and Skylar finishing their breakfast.

Everyone laughed, but Dale felt as if there was a lump in his throat. He was sad on the inside, but he could not let Katherine know he was saying goodbye. He stayed around for a while and then went back home.

Dale went to his apartment, took all the money he had saved, and his money as a cadet. He had no use for it, so he boxed it, put shipping tape on the box, and wrote a note saying it was for Stanley Hall.

Dale also wrote a note to Rodney about his truck and the Bel Air, saying he wanted him to have both. He also asked Rodney to take care of Sir Mozart.

He joined Rodney as he was cleaning the garage. It was only three o'clock, and Dale felt he could not face any more of his friends. He was having a tough time containing his emotions. He cleaned the apartment and went to Webb's Mill, where he sat until well after dark.

At ten o'clock, Dale parked beside E. H.'s truck, got out, and headed to Blackstone. He had previously told E. H. not to come to the landing area, and E. H. had complied with Dale's wishes.

Dale stood near the spot where nothing grows until he heard the low-pitched hum of the craft. He then walked head down towards the landing area, thinking, I never knew it would hurt so much to love someone. How can an emotion hurt you physically? I feel so empty and guilty. I should have never let anyone get close to me. How can pure love turn to excruciating pain, and how do I endure the pain? I won't have Rex to confide in. Oh, my friend, I still and always will miss you; until they wipe my brain clean.

Suddenly, Dale heard someone calling his name. He looked back. There was no one there. He turned around and saw a cadet brother standing in front of him. Dale said, "Where did you come from?"

The cadet did not speak. He held a folded piece of paper and motioned for Dale to take it. When Dale took the letter, the cadet said in French, "ouvrir cette."

EPISODE 73

Dale opened the letter as directed and silently read the words: "Your mission changed to a permanent assignment. Wheels are turning for you, Cadet Dale Weaver.

Go back to doing what you have been doing and wait. Events are unfolding which will one day make you an essential citizen of Blackstone County. We promote you to full-time Earth Cadet for so long as you shall live. Signed, Federation of Planets.

When Dale looked back up, his cadet brother had retreated and was already inside the craft. Dale watched the craft rise and go out of sight. He now knew what the gray letter meant when it said, "Be Ready."

Dale turned and walked back to the Denton home, got into his truck, and drove to his apartment. He destroyed the letter to Rodney and unwrapped the package for Stanley.

Dale looked out the window into the darkness, took out his cell phone, and called E. H.

NOT THE END

BLACKSTONE COUNTY MISSION TWO

IS WAITING FOR YOU